1

For Jasper:
For dropkicking me into this mad
world of books, I owe you a debt of gratitude.

CHAPTER ONE

Peter Ashe made the sign of the cross and took a seat facing the screen in front of him.

"May God who has enlightened every heart," Father Swift began. "Help you to know your sins and trust in his mercy."

"Forgive me, father for I have sinned. It's been so long since my last confession that I cannot remember when it was."

"You're here now," Father Swift told him.

The confessional booth was silent for a moment. Father Swift waited for Peter to continue.

"These are my sins," he spoke eventually and the booth became quiet again. After a few seconds Peter Ashe confessed. "I have lied to my wife – not once but on many occasions, and I have sought the comfort of other women."

"Go on," Father Swift said calmly.

"It has been going on for some time now, and I wanted to stop but I couldn't."

"Have you spoken with your wife about these transgressions?"

"Only when she found out," David admitted. "I don't know what to do about it."

"The fact that you are here today is an indication that you want to make amends. With your wife, and more importantly with God."

"There's more, father," Peter Ashe's voice had risen slightly in pitch. "I knew it was wrong, but I gave in to temptation. And in doing so I broke the law. I don't know if I can tell you anymore than that."

"The law has no business in my church," Father Swift assured him.

He spent the next twenty minutes listening to Peter Ashe's confession. When he was finished Peter let out a loud sigh.

"What do I do, Father?" he asked.

"Is this unlawful *relationship* still ongoing?"

"No," Peter replied at once. "It's over, but my wife refuses to forgive me. She won't even talk to me."

"Forgiveness does not happen overnight," Father Swift said. "It takes time. You have owned up to your sins and now the hard part begins. You need to give your wife some time and only then can you start to make peace with everything. God, your wife, and most importantly yourself."

When Peter Ashe walked away from St Olave's Church on Marygate the weight he'd been carrying that morning felt lighter. He knew he had a long road ahead of him before his transgressions could be truly forgiven, but he felt like he'd taken the first step, and he was determined to do whatever it took to make things right.

What Peter Ashe didn't realise was it was already too late for that. Much too late.

* * *

Three miles away in a terraced house outside the city, a man had just switched off a machine that consisted of a receiver, an amplifier and a speaker. The receiver was linked to a recording device hidden in the confessional booth at St Olave's Church, and the man had just finished listening to the conversation between Father Swift and Peter Ashe.

What Peter Ashe also didn't realise was the penance for his sins was to be a great deal worse than he ever could have imagined.

CHAPTER TWO

Detective Sergeant Jason Smith stared at the three-year-old girl in the small bed. He'd been there for quite some time. His wife, Detective Constable Erica Whitton was still asleep in their bedroom, and Smith was looking forward to the first weekend off as a family for as long as he could remember. Laura, their daughter started to stir. She opened her eyes and gazed up at her Dad.

"Good morning, beautiful," Smith said and moved closer to take in her scent. He never tired of his daughter's aroma. She held out both hands and Smith took her in his arms.

"Let's go and wake that mother of yours, shall we?"

Whitton was already awake.

She rubbed her eyes. "What time is it?"

"Half-eight," Smith told her. "So if we don't get some food inside this child soon, all hell is going to break loose."

He held Laura's hand as she navigated the stairs. One by one she carefully stepped down until they reached the bottom.

"Break-cats," she said.

"I'm going to make breakfast now," Smith told her and left her to make her own way to the kitchen.

He boiled a couple of eggs and sat Laura in her chair. He switched on the kettle to make coffee and let the dogs out the back door. Theakston, the Bull Terrier was getting old and lazy and slowly ambled out into the garden. Fred, the repulsive Pug was much livelier. Smith followed them out and lit a cigarette. It was early April – there was still a nip in the air, but there wasn't a cloud in the sky. He inhaled deeply and blew out a cloud of smoke. They were planning on driving across to Bridlington for a day by the sea. They were determined to make the most of their first weekend off together in weeks.

Smith finished his cigarette and went back inside. Whitton had made two cups of coffee. Laura had already finished her breakfast.

"That child has some appetite," Smith said to Whitton. "She definitely gets that from her mother. The weather looks good. It's not that warm but the sky's clear. This is going to be just what the doctor ordered."

"Says he who used to hate the sea," Whitton said.

"I didn't hate it," Smith pointed out. "I had a bit of a phobia – there's a big difference, and I'm over that now. Do you think she's had enough food? It's a forty minute drive to Bridlington."

"I'm sure she'll survive," Whitton laughed. "I'll pack some fruit for the car."

At nine-thirty they were ready to go. Smith had just kicked the dogs out into the back garden and locked the back door when his phone started to ring on the kitchen table.

He ignored it and left it where it was. The ringing stopped then immediately started again.

"Aren't you going to answer that?" Whitton asked.

"That phone only brings bad news."

"Just see who it is," Whitton said. "We're both off this weekend, so if it's work just remind them of that."

Smith gave in and looked at the screen. "It's Yang Chu."

"Answer it," Whitton insisted.

Smith pressed, *answer*. "Yang Chu, what's so urgent you have to bother me on the first weekend off I've had in weeks?"

"Sorry, Sarge," the young DC said. "But I think you need to hear this. There's been a murder. A pretty nasty one."

"All murders are nasty, Yang Chu. And how many times do I have to remind you I am not the only Police Detective in York?"

"We're short-staffed, Sarge – what with you and Whitton off and with what happened to Brownhill."

Detective Inspector Bryony Brownhill had been killed earlier in the year and they had not yet replaced her.

"You and Bridge can deal with it," Smith was starting to get annoyed.

"Bridge is off sick with a nasty cold."

"Nasty hangover more like," Smith scoffed. "OK, what have we got?"

Whitton glared at him and Smith had to look away.

"Like I said, Sarge," Yang Chu told him. "It's a really nasty one, and I think you'd better come and have a look for yourself."

He gave Smith the address.

"You're not going to do what I think you're going to do are you?" Whitton said when Smith had ended the call.

"Yang Chu is on his own," Smith explained. "Bridge is off sick, and to be honest there's nobody else I'd trust to step in this early in an investigation."

"You promised. You promised work wouldn't be your main priority anymore. After everything that has happened, I can't believe you're going to break that promise."

"I'll be an hour at the most," Smith said. "I'll go and check out the scene and leave Yang Chu and whoever else is there to carry on. You know how important the initial stages are. We'll head off to Bridlington when I get back."

"I've heard that one before," Whitton said and took hold of Laura's hand. "Come on. Let's go out to the back garden and get some fresh air while we wait for your Daddy to come back from his crusade."

Whitton's scathing words were still fresh in Smith's ears as he drove towards the address Yang Chu had given him.

Crusade? He thought that was a bit harsh.

He made a mental note to have a few words with DS Bridge when he got the chance. He thought the promotion would have made Bridge grow up a bit, but holding the rank of Detective Sergeant didn't appear to make a blind bit of difference to Bridge's womanising and boozing.

Smith parked the car outside the house in one of the new housing estates just outside the city. The house was a modern semi-detached property with a decent-sized front garden. Two police cars and an ambulance were parked outside, as was Yang Chu's Ford Focus. Smith got out of his car just as Grant Webber pulled up in front of him. The Head of Forensics got out and Smith gasped. Since the death of DI Brownhill, Webber had taken strain but the man who walked up to Smith now looked like one of the living dead. His face was deathly pale, and his red-rimmed eyes were sunken into their sockets. He had also lost a considerable amount of weight.

"Morning, Webber," Smith said. "Are you alright? You don't look too healthy."

"I can't sleep," Webber said. "I don't think I've slept more than a few hours non-stop since it happened."

Smith patted him on the shoulder. "It gets easier. I promise you it does get easier."

"What have we got?" Webber nodded to indicate Smith's empathy was appreciated but it was now time to get down to business.

"I've only just got here. Me and Whitton were supposed to have a weekend off, but Yang Chu told me they're short-staffed. Bridge is off sick."

Webber rolled his eyes. "Let's go and see what's waiting for us in there then, shall we?"

CHAPTER THREE

Smith went inside the house and was greeted by Yang Chu in the hallway. "Sorry to cut your weekend short, Sarge," he said. "But I thought you should see this. He's lying in the living room."

Smith walked past him and stopped in the doorway. His SOC suit was starting to itch. He scratched his arm and went inside the room.

A man was lying on his back in the middle of the carpet. His eyes were wide open as was his mouth. A long ornate, wooden knife handle was sticking out of his chest over his heart. His light-blue shirt was dotted with blood. There was another larger blood stain on his trousers just below the waist. Webber came in with Yang Chu.

"Looks like that's what killed him," Smith pointed to the knife. "Straight into the heart. He probably died instantly. It's an unusual-looking knife. Do we know who he is yet?"

"Peter Ashe," Yang Chu replied. "It was his wife who called it in. They've been having some marriage problems and she's been staying with her sister. She came back to fetch a few things this morning and that's when she found him."

"Where is she now?" Smith asked. "The wife?"

"With her sister. She took it pretty badly and she's been given a sedative. I doubt we'll be able to get much more out of her for the time being."

Smith started to walk around the room. There was a huge television fixed to one of the walls – a bookcase filled with paperbacks stood against another wall and a desk with a laptop computer on it filled one corner. The room was clean and very tidy.

"What are you thinking?" Webber asked.

"Does this look like a typical murder scene to you?" Smith said.

"I don't think there is such a thing. But you're right. I'll need to have a closer look, but there doesn't appear to be anything out of place. There's nothing to indicate that any kind of struggle took place in here at all."

"And I don't think it was a burglary gone wrong," Smith added. "That laptop looks like it's worth a few bob. We'll need to check the rest of the house of course, but it doesn't look like there was anything taken."

A man Smith didn't recognise came in. He was carrying a Scene of Crime case.

"Smith," Webber said. "This is Harry – he's just joined my team and I'm expecting great things from him."

Smith nodded to him. "Pleased to meet you. I'll leave you in peace. I just want to have a look around the rest of the house."

Webber opened his mouth to speak but Smith got there first.

"I promise I won't touch anything."

He and Yang Chu walked back towards the front door. It had a lock that automatically locked itself without needing to use a key. The locking mechanism was intact and there was no indication it had been forced in any way.

"This wasn't a break in gone wrong," Smith said. "My first impression here is that Mr Ashe knew the person who killed him. No sign of a struggle inside, no indication of forced entry to the house. Nothing. Webber is going to be busy for a while, and we'll know more when the initial path report comes in, but right now we need to focus on one thing."

"Motive," Yang Chu said.

Smith smiled. "Am I really that predictable?"

"Afraid so, Sarge."

"We'll need to speak to his wife as soon as she's able to talk – you mentioned something about marriage problems. That could be relevant."

"She could be the killer," Yang Chu pointed out.

"She's my number one suspect at the moment," Smith told him. "She has a key for the place – they were having personal problems, and he wouldn't be expecting her to attack him. She could have killed him without him even knowing what was happening. We need to find out more about this man."

Smith suddenly remembered something. Whitton and Laura were waiting for him at home. He'd promised he would only be away for an hour. He stepped outside into the fresh air, lit a cigarette and took out his phone.

"Is this the famous *I can't get away* phone call?" Whitton spoke first.

"I'm sorry," Smith said. "I really can't get away. This really is a bizarre one. They're so short-staffed I can't just leave Yang Chu and Webber on their own. Why don't you and Laura head across to Bridlington without me?"

"I suppose we could do that. She's really been looking forward to it. Is it really that bad?"

"As far as cause of death – I've seen worse, but it's the crime scene that's puzzling. No sign of a break in, no indication that a struggle took place inside and the murder weapon has been left behind."

"That is odd," Whitton agreed. "I suppose you don't know what time you'll be finished?"

"You know what it's like. Have a great time by the sea."

"We will."

"And, Whitton?"

"Yes?"

"Bring me back a stick of rock."

Smith went back inside the house. Webber was talking to his technician in the kitchen.

"Find anything?" Smith asked Webber.

"Give us a chance," Webber said and rubbed the stubble on his chin. "We've only been here five minutes."

"We found a mobile phone connected to a charger on the wall," Harry, Webber's technician said. "But it's got a fingerprint lock and we don't know the override password."

Webber grinned at Smith as though he knew what was coming next.

"Your fingerprint is in there," Smith pointed to the door that led to the living room. "Attached to a bloke with a knife in his heart. I'm sure he won't mind if you use it to open his phone."

Harry stared at Smith, wide-eyed.

"Do as he says," Webber said. "Welcome to the team."

Harry returned a short while later with the phone. "I used his thumbprint."

He handed the phone to Smith and Smith opened it up.

"Two phone calls yesterday afternoon from the same number," he said. "We'll get them checked. No more calls after that. We'll have more idea of the TOD when pathology has finished. What do you think, Webber?"

"I'd make a rough guess he died sometime last night. Corneal turbidity was well advanced, and rigor has started to set in. Livor mortis is evident on the skin at the back of the neck, so, unless his heating was turned right up and the killer turned it off, I'd put it at sometime between six pm and midnight yesterday."

"These phone calls were received at half-past-four," Smith told him. "And it shows that someone answered the calls. Of course, it could have been our killer for all we know, but from your initial pathology report I don't think it was."

"I'm just going on experience," Webber said. "I'm no Pathologist."

"I'm inclined to agree with you," Smith said and opened up the Messenger App. "He received a message at eight last night. The message hasn't been read yet."

Smith read the message, frowned and read it again.

"What does it say?" Webber asked.

Smith handed him the phone.

"*God has forgiven you your sins*," Webber read. "*But He could not rid you of your demons, so I've taken them for you.*"

CHAPTER FOUR

"What do you think it means?" Yang Chu asked Smith back at the station.

"*God has forgiven you your sins,*" Smith read off the piece of paper in front of him. "*But He could not rid you of your demons*. I haven't got a clue. We don't even know if it's relevant to the investigation."

DCI Bob Chalmers came into the canteen and headed straight for the coffee machine in the corner. He pressed a few buttons, a loud gurgling sound was heard and then nothing.

"Does either of you two know how this bloody machine works?" He addressed the question in the direction of Smith and Yang Chu.

"Give it a good whack, sir," Yang Chu suggested. "Right on the side there."

Chalmers did as Yang Chu suggested, a paper cup appeared and was slowly filled with a mysterious brown liquid.

"What are you doing here on a weekend, boss?" Smith asked when Chalmers sat down.

"I've been coming in to get some paperwork done for a few weekends now," Chalmers replied. "It's the only time I can get some peace without old Smyth breathing down my neck. You know the Super won't show his face on a Saturday or Sunday unless there's a chance to star in a press conference. Anyway, I could ask you the same question. Didn't you and Whitton have a weekend off together?"

Smith told him about the murder of Peter Ashe.

"Any leads so far?" Chalmers asked when Smith was finished.

"It was his wife who found him," Smith said. "So we'll have more when we've spoken to her, but she's pretty much out of it right now. She was given a sedative."

"No sign of a break-in?" Chalmers said.

"Nothing to suggest it, boss," Smith said. "The locks on both the front and back doors were intact, and there were no broken windows anywhere. No, I'd say Mr Ashe knew the person who did this."

"Smith's gunning for the wife at the moment, sir," Yang Chu joined in.

"I'm not gunning for anyone, Yang Chu," Smith glared at him. "She's the one who found him – she has a key to the house, and they just happened to be having marriage problems. Therefore, she is the first person we're going to speak to, if only to rule her out. Right now, I want to have a closer look at Peter Ashe himself."

"Motive?" Chalmers said.

"Exactly. We've got to wait for the forensics and path reports, so it's all we have for the time being."

"Have you seen Webber recently, boss?" Smith changed the subject. "He looks terrible."

"I went round there the other night," Chalmers said. "Him and the DI were very close – he told me they'd even talked about getting married, and he's taking what happened to her very badly. He'll come out of it alright. He just needs a bit more time. I'd better be getting back to work. Let me know if you need any help with this one. I realise we're a bit short-staffed right now and it would be good to get my hands dirty for a change."

"Will do, boss," Smith told him.

"What now then, Sarge?" Yang Chu asked. "This doesn't feel right if you ask me."

"How do you mean?" Smith said.

"A man has just been murdered, and what are York Police actually doing about it? Bridge is allowed to stay at home with a stupid cold – Whitton is lapping up the sea air, and we're sitting around drinking coffee. This wouldn't be happening if Brownhill was still around. I realised the other day that I actually really miss her."

DI Brownhill had only been dead a matter of weeks. She'd been following up a lead on a case involving an *artist* who killed her victims to take their blood to use in art, when she stumbled upon the killer by accident. She was tied up and most of the blood circulating around her body was drained. By the time Smith and the team arrived it was too late. The DI had lost far too much blood and there was nothing they could do for her.

"You're right," Smith said. "Of course, you're right. The first thing we need to do is find out more about the victim, Peter Ashe, and I'm afraid that means speaking to the woman who found him."

"His wife has been sedated, Sarge," Yang Chu reminded him.

"Then she'll be quite calm when we talk to her," Smith said. "Let's go."

Peter Ashe's sister-in-law lived a short distance away from where Peter Ashe lived. Smith and Yang Chu rang the doorbell and the door was opened a short while later by an angry-looking woman with more piercings in her face than Smith had ever seen before. Smith thought she looked like she'd had an accident in a staple factory.

"What do you want?" She demanded and revealed another couple of studs in her tongue.

"Police," Smith took out his ID. "Detectives' Smith and Yang Chu. We need to speak to Mrs Ashe."

"Naomi is still groggy from the drugs she was given," she said.

"It is extremely important we talk to her," Smith said. "I'm not sure if you are aware but the first twenty-four-hours in a murder investigation are crucial."

As soon as the words left his lips, he realised how hypocritical it sounded. If the first twenty-four hours were so crucial why was it that only he, Yang Chu and Grant Webber were busy with the investigation?

"We realise this is a difficult time," Smith added. "Mrs?"

"Miss," the woman said. "Penelope Slyper. Do we have a choice?"

"Yes," Smith admitted. "But it would help us out if we could just talk with Mrs Ashe for a few minutes."

Penelope led them inside a small but tidy living room. A woman was sitting in an armchair at the opposite side of the room. If it wasn't for the glazed look in her eyes and the absence of metal in her face she could easily be mistaken for her sister. They were almost identical. There was a peculiar smell in the room.

Smith took a seat on a three-seater next to her, and Yang Chu sat next to Smith.

"Mrs Ashe," Smith began. "I know this is difficult, but I'm from the York Police and I'd like to ask you a few questions. Do you think you can manage that?"

Heidi Ashe looked at him and nodded.

"Good," Smith said. "You were the one who found Peter. Is that right?"

Another nod.

"Can you remember roughly what time that was?"

"Around eight-thirty," she replied.

Smith thought back to that morning. At eight-thirty he'd been giving Laura her breakfast, then Whitton had woken up and they got everything ready for their trip to the coast. He arrived at Peter Ashe's house just before ten. Heidi Ashe must have phoned the police straight away after she found her husband.

Smith made a mental note to bring that up later.

"What did you do?" he asked. "When you saw him lying there?"

"I phoned the police," she said. "What do you think I did?"

"When was the last time you saw your husband?" Yang Chu said.

"I saw him the day before yesterday. I went round to fetch some things I needed."

"So, Thursday then?"

"Right."

"And you didn't see him at all yesterday?"

"I told you, the last time I saw him was on Thursday."

"We need to ask you this, Mrs Ashe," Smith said. "Where were you yesterday? Let's say between 4pm and midnight?"

"Is my sister a suspect here?" Penelope asked.

"Please just answer the question, Mrs Ashe," Smith spoke in a soft voice.

"I was here. I was here all afternoon. I went into town in the morning, but I came back around noon and I didn't go out again. Penny will confirm it."

"It's true," Penelope said.

"OK, Mrs Ashe," Smith continued, "Do you know if Peter had any enemies? Can you think of anybody who would want to do this to him?"

It was as though somebody had sent a jolt of electricity through her body. Her eyes brightened and her face appeared more alert.

"If you'd asked me that a week ago, I would have told you I wanted to kill him myself."

"Go on."

"I haven't got it in me though. But I hated him."

"Why did you hate him?"

"You don't have to tell them anything," Penelope cast her sister a hard stare.

"It's alright," Heidi said. "I knew Peter was a bastard when I married him. I knew all about his wandering eye, and I could tolerate most of it, but when I found out about that little tart, that was the final straw."

"Mrs Ashe?" Smith urged.

"He said he didn't know how old she was," she said. "If he'd known he wouldn't have gone anywhere near her, but I knew he was lying. They kill people like him in prison all the time. I've read about it in the papers."

"People like him?"

"Perverts," Heidi elaborated. "Last week I found out that my husband was having an affair with a fourteen-year-old schoolgirl."

CHAPTER FIVE

"Well that was quite a revelation," Yang Chu said as he and Smith drove away from Penelope Slyper's house.

"It most certainly was," Smith agreed. "And I've got a feeling it was a revelation that is extremely relevant to this investigation."

"Did you see all those piercings? Why would someone want to do that to themselves? I bet she has fun with the metal detectors at the airport. What's the plan?"

Smith was about to reply when the sound of his phone ringing interrupted his thoughts.

He turned on the hands-free. "Smith."

"Detective." It was Dr Kenny Bean. "I hope your breakfast is fully digested because I've got something for you that might make you wish you hadn't eaten anything this morning."

"Good afternoon to you too, Kenny," Smith said to the eccentric Head of Pathology. "What have you got?"

"Not over the phone. This is far too delicate a matter to discuss over the airwaves. How soon can you get to the hospital?"

"We're about five minutes away."

"Splendid. You're going to want to hear this."

"Why does he always have to be so vague?" Yang Chu asked when Smith switched off the hands-free. "Why can't he just come out with what he's found?"

"He's a pathologist," Smith explained. "He spends his days around the dead, so you can't deny him a bit of drama and suspense. You never met The Ghoul did you?"

"Before my time, Sarge."

"Now he was a character. Not everyone's cup of tea, but he was always entertaining to be around. I reckon you'd go mad cutting up dead bodies if you didn't inject a bit of humour into it once in a while. I wonder what he's found."

* * *

Dr Kenny Bean keyed in a code on a key pad next to the door to his office and beckoned for Smith and Yang Chu to go inside.

"Take a seat," he said. "I've run out of coffee, so you're out of luck on that front."

"We've not long had one," Smith said. "You've found something interesting, haven't you?"

Dr Bean sat opposite them and leaned back in his chair with his hands behind his head.

"Kenny," Smith said. "This is a murder investigation – we haven't got time for games."

"You're getting old and boring," Dr Bean said and looked at Yang Chu. "Don't you think he's getting old and boring?"

"No comment," Yang Chu said with a smile on his face.

"Kenny," Smith urged.

"Right," Dr Bean sat up straighter in his chair. "We've only done a preliminary examination – the poor man was only brought in a few hours ago, but I can tell you a number of things from that examination. Firstly, it wasn't the knife piercing the heart that killed him."

"Are you sure?" Yang Chu said and instantly regretted it.

"I'll put that down to a case of the mouth working before the brain has a chance to stop it," Dr Bean said.

"Sorry," Yang Chu offered.

"Go on," Smith said. "What killed him then?"

"This is what I didn't want to discuss over the phone," Dr Bean said. "Especially when I deduced from the background noise that you were driving. There's no possible way to candy-coat this. The poor man had his manhood removed."

"What?" Yang Chu exclaimed.

"His manhood," Dr Bean said once more. "Whatever you want to call it – his penis, cock, dick, one-eyed trouser snake, it was cut off at the base."

Smith and Yang Chu both crossed their legs at the same time.

Dr Bean chuckled. "I must admit I had the same reaction when I made the gruesome discovery. Any man's worst nightmare, wouldn't you agree?"

"And that was what killed him?" Yang Chu asked.

"I believe it was. I'll try and explain this in layman's terms. The composition of the penis is such that the arteries tend to dilate more than the other arteries in the body, and veins tend to constrict more. A trauma such as a total removal of the organ would lead to a bleed that would be continuous. The arteries inside the member, and leading to it very rarely clamp off."

"Good God," Smith said. "What a way to go. Do you have a rough estimate on the time of death?"

"Very rough at this stage. I can narrow it down to a window of three hours or so. If I take everything into consideration, I'd say his heart stopped beating sometime between 6pm and 9pm yesterday. I'll have more for you when we've completed more tests but I knew you'd want to know the grim details about the poor man's todger."

"Thanks, Kenny," Smith said. "I think."

Dr Bean's office was silent for a moment. All three men in the room seemed to be digesting the shocking fate that had befallen Peter Ashe. It was Smith who broke the silence. "If he died from having his penis amputated, that means he was still alive when it happened."

"You're not normally someone who can be accused of stating the obvious, my friend," Dr Bean said.

"That's not what I'm getting at. If he was alive when it was lopped off, how did they do it? We were at the crime scene earlier this morning and there was no sign whatsoever that any kind of struggle took place. I'm sure you'll agree with me, if you knew you were about to get your pride and joy chopped off you wouldn't just lie back and let it happen would you?"

"Do you think he was drugged first?" Yang Chu suggested.

"There's a good chance that he was," Smith said. "Dr Bean?"

"I'll prioritise it. If we find anything in his system that should not be there I promise you, you will be the first to know."

CHAPTER SIX

"What a horrible way to die," Yang Chu said and got out of Smith's car. Smith had dropped him back at the station to retrieve his car.

"I can't think of a worse way to die," Yang Chu added.

"I'll see you tomorrow," Smith said. "We've got a mountain of stuff to go over – Dr Bean should have more for us, and I'm sure Webber will be able to give us something too, so we're going to need all hands on deck. Cold or no cold, Bridge is going to be at work. Mine and Whitton's weekend is officially cancelled, and I want to get Baldwin on the team again. We need as many minds as we can muster on this one. Keep your legs crossed, and don't have nightmares."

"Thanks a lot, Sarge," Yang Chu grimaced. "I'll see you bright and early in the morning."

Whitton and Laura were still not back when Smith went inside the house and he felt a pang of guilt when he realised he was glad of it. After what had happened in the last few hours he needed some peace and quiet to process everything. He knew that as soon as his wife and daughter burst through the door, all talk would be of seagulls, candy floss and sandcastles, and there would be no way he would be able to concentrate on the recent murder.

He took a beer out of the fridge and opened the back door. As soon as he stepped outside he was besieged by two excited dogs.

"Hey, boys," he said to Theakston and Fred. "What have you been up to today?"

It was a rhetorical question as Smith knew only too well that as soon as the dogs heard the key in the back door they would have made themselves comfortable in the shade and very soon a snoring contest would have ensued. Smith lit a cigarette and sat down on the wooden bench. He took a long swig of beer and thought hard about what Kenny Bean had told them.

Peter Ashe was still alive when his penis was amputated. Who would do such a thing and what did it mean? He knew instinctively that it was symbolic. He had never heard of anybody killing someone in that manner before. Stabbing him in the heart would have had the same end result.

"Somebody wanted Peter Ashe to die," Smith spoke out loud. "But they wanted him and the rest of the world to understand why he had to die."

Smith realised at once it was the *why* he had to die that they needed to concentrate on. And he also knew that the information Peter's wife had given them was extremely important.

He was having an affair with a fourteen-year-old schoolgirl.

Smith shivered at the thought. He finished his beer and went inside to get another one. The front door opened and Whitton and Laura came inside.

"You missed out on a great day," Whitton said and dumped Laura's day-bag on the carpet next to the stairs. "We had fish and chips on a bench overlooking the sea. Laura loved it. She's knackered now, though. Is everything alright?"

"I'll tell you about it later," Smith said and kissed her on the cheek. "Let's get Laura settled first – it's not exactly suitable for the ears of a child."

Whitton nodded and a concerned look appeared on her face. "Are you OK?"

"I don't know," Smith admitted. "And I'm afraid the weekend off is cancelled. Do you think your parents can have Laura tomorrow?"

"Of course. You know they love having her around."

An hour or so later, Smith and Whitton sat outside in the back garden. Smith had given Laura a bath and now she was fast asleep dreaming about the waves lapping on the beach.

"Was it that bad?" Whitton asked.

"Like I said," Smith said. "The murder scene itself didn't faze me much, but it was what we found out later that's really disturbing. Firstly, the dead bloke's wife told us he was having an affair with a fourteen-year-old."

"You're kidding me. How old was he?"

"He was twenty-nine, but it's what Kenny Bean discovered that really made me sick. The bloke had his penis cut off, and he was still alive when it happened."

"Oh my God. Who would do such a thing?"

"That's what I'm going to find out."

"What about his wife?" Whitton said. "I've heard of stories where women find out about their husband's cheating and see red and chop off their man's thing."

"She was with her sister all afternoon," Smith said. "And I think there's more to it than that. This wasn't a spur of the moment thing – it was well-planned, and the fact he was left to bleed to death and then stabbed in the heart doesn't make any sense."

"This is just awful."

"I want a full team on it first thing in the morning. Us, Bridge, Yang Chu and Baldwin. She's proven be very resourceful in the past. Oh, and the DCI has offered to lend a hand."

"Chalmers?" Whitton laughed. "And how's he planning on escaping the Super?"

"Chalmers has the measure of old Smyth. He'll think of something. All I know is we've got a lot to go through tomorrow. Now, can we talk about something else? Is Bridlington still as tacky as ever?"

"It's not tacky. And Laura absolutely loved it. You should see how much they've cleaned the place up since we were last there. They have litter bins everywhere now. We took a long walk along the beach, and Laura chased the waves for ages. Then we had fish and chips from a quaint little shop in the old town. We took them down to the beachfront and ate them out of a newspaper. The seagulls were a nuisance as usual. Laura was horrified when one almost made off with one of her chips."

"I bet," Smith smiled. "You do not come between that child and her food."

Whitton continued to tell him about everything. She didn't leave anything out. Smith listened contently. He was grateful for a distraction from the horrors he'd witnessed during the day. He'd think about that tomorrow. Tomorrow was not his problem right now.

CHAPTER SEVEN

Tomorrow arrived much too soon for Smith's liking. It felt as though no sooner had he said good night to Whitton, than the alarm on his mobile phone was blaring in his ear.

Now they sat in the small conference room. Yang Chu sat next to PC Baldwin. DS Bridge had yet to make an appearance as had Grant Webber and DCI Chalmers.

"This looks like it for today," Smith said scanning the faces at the table. "Oh well, four minds are better than none."

The door opened and Grant Webber came in with Bridge. As soon as Smith saw Bridge's red nose and puffy eyes he felt guilty for doubting his fellow Detective Sergeant's excuses for not coming to work the day before.

"Sorry I'm late," Webber said. "I overslept."

Bridge sniffed. "What's the urgency? I should be in bed – this is the worst cold I've had in years."

"Let's make a start," Smith assumed command and the silence in the room told him that nobody had any objections.

"As I'm sure you're all aware, the body of a man was found by his wife yesterday morning at around eight-thirty. This man has been identified as Peter Ashe, a twenty-nine-year old refuse collector. His wife found him in the middle of the living room with a knife in his heart. Early path reports put the time of death between 6pm and 9pm on Friday. We'll have a more detailed time when Dr Bean is finished, but that's what we've got to go on at the moment. Before I continue, Grant, are we any further with forensics?"

Webber opened up a file in front of him. "No sign of forced entry into the property. The locks on both the front and back doors were intact and there were no windows broken. In the living room, where the body was discovered, we found samples of hair but until we've compared them with Mr

Ashe and his wife, we won't know whether they're relevant. Nothing untoward upstairs. It doesn't appear that anything was taken, so we can probably rule out a burglary gone wrong. Once again, until Mrs Ashe has checked to see if anything is missing, we can't be positive there either."

"What about the murder weapon?" Bridge was obviously more awake than he looked.

"Unusual knife," Webber said. "We're still busy with it but I can tell you I've never seen anything like it. Very thin pointed blade and a rather exquisite wooden handle. It bears more resemblance to a fire poker than a knife, but it was sharp enough to pierce his heart."

"That's not the murder weapon," Smith said and everybody besides Yang Chu turned to look at him.

The way Webber had described the knife that was sticking out of Peter Ashe's chest reinforced what Kenny Bean had said. It wasn't the knife that killed Ashe.

"Peter Ashe was already dead when he was stabbed," he said.

He went on to describe exactly what happened to Peter Ashe. When he was finished nobody spoke.

"What we need to work out," Smith took the initiative. "Is why would somebody do this?"

"It's the wife," Bridge offered. "He was probably playing away from home and she found out about it."

"You're not too far off the mark there," Smith said. "It turns out that Mr Ashe was indeed conducting an extra-marital relationship, but not in the usual sense of the word."

"What do you mean?" Baldwin spoke for the first time.

"His wife found out he was having an affair with a fourteen-year-old," Smith told her.

"A schoolgirl?" Bridge said. "Bloody hell."

"And the wife has an alibi for the time of death," Smith added. "So we can rule out that possibility."

"A fourteen-year-old girl," Bridge said once more. "What the hell was he playing at?"

"It still doesn't explain why his member was amputated," Whitton pointed out. "Why do that?"

"Could be the girl's father," Baldwin suggested. "Maybe he found out about the affair and chopped off the culprit's thingy."

"Thingy?" Bridge said. "Who the hell calls it a *thingy*? Besides, a man wouldn't do that. It's out of the question. It strikes me as more something a woman would do. Us blokes are quite particular about our tackle."

"Right," Smith needed to steer the briefing in another direction. "This is the plan of action. Bridge, seeing as you're a bit under the weather, I want you to go through the National Database to find out if anything similar to this jumps out at you. Baldwin can help you. Whitton, you and Yang Chu can go and speak to Mrs Ashe again. At the risk of sounding sexist, I think she might open up a bit more with a woman present."

"That's not sexist at all," Whitton said.

"Ask her about the affair with the young girl. Find out if anybody else knew about it."

"What about you, Sarge?" Yang Chu said.

"I'm going to find out who this schoolgirl is and go and speak with her."

"I'll come with you," DCI Chalmers had entered the room. "There's something I need to discuss with you anyway so we might as well kill two birds with one stone.

CHAPTER EIGHT

"I'm getting a slight sense of déjà vu here, boss," Smith said as he turned the key in the ignition. "I seem to recall having this conversation once before."

"But that was different," Chalmers said. "That was when your head was in a bad space. You've come a long way since then. The job is yours – you just have to give me the nod, and I'll get the ball rolling."

Chalmers had just informed him that the Detective Inspector post was up for grabs and it was Smith's if he wanted it.

"I'm happy to stay a DS," Smith said. "I told you that then, and I'm sticking to it."

"Think about it," Chalmers wasn't giving up. "Think about the big picture. With you as a DI, a DS position will open up, and who do you think is most qualified for that?"

"Whitton, I suppose."

"You suppose? She'll make a bloody good DS. Two promotions for the price of one. She wasn't ready last time – what with the baby just being born, but now she is. Just think about what a difference that will make to your household income."

"I'm happy to stay a DS," Smith said once more. "Now, can we talk about something else?"

"You're a bloody stubborn idiot sometimes. Just promise me you'll at least give it some consideration."

"I'll have a think about it," Smith relented. "The girl's place is just around the corner."

When the door to the address they'd been given for Louise Platt was opened, Smith found himself stepping back a few paces. The man in front of him filled the doorway. He had to be almost seven feet tall and big with it. He had a very friendly face.

He smiled at Smith and Chalmers. "Can I help you?"

"Mr Platt," Smith said. "We're from the York Police. Can we have a word?"

"Of course. Come inside."

He shifted his considerable bulk out of their way and gestured with his hand for them to come in.

"Come through to the living room. Can I get you anything to drink?"

"No thank you," Smith replied.

"Is this about Ashe?" Platt came straight to the point.

They all sat down in the living room. Platt eased himself onto a huge armchair that Smith thought had to have been custom-made to hold his weight. The sound of music could be heard from upstairs.

"Why would you assume that?" Chalmers said and sat down.

"I heard what happened," Platt said. "News travels fast with all the local gossips. I'm afraid I can't say I'm sorry."

"And why is that?" Smith asked.

"Because of what the man is or was. It's a terrible thing to happen, but I'm not in the slightest bit sorry about it. Louise is devastated – she's barely come out of her room since she found out."

"Louise is your daughter?" Chalmers said.

"Yes, and that bastard took advantage of her. You know how impressionable fourteen-year-olds are. It's disgusting what he did."

"Mr Platt," Smith said. "Are you telling us you knew about your daughter's relationship with this man?"

"I only found out after it had been going on for a while," Platt told them.

"And what did you do?" Chalmers asked. "What did you do when you found out?"

"I sat Louise down and we had a long chat. We have a very open father-daughter relationship, Louise and I, especially since her mother died, and we can talk about anything."

"Did you confront Mr Ashe about the affair?" Chalmers asked.

"I know what you're thinking," Platt said. "What kind of father am I? Why didn't I go straight round there and beat the living daylights out of the man?"

"Something like that," Chalmers admitted.

"And what good would that have done? I spoke to him calmly and explained to him that not only was what they were doing illegal, it was immoral. And it had to stop."

"And how did he take that?" Smith said.

"He agreed. He agreed to back off."

"What about Louise?" Chalmers said.

"Louise took it badly. She really believed they were in love and they were going to live happily ever after. Everything is blown out of proportion at that age. You must remember that."

"When was the last time you saw Mr Ashe?" Smith asked.

"I only spoke to him once, and that was just over a week ago. Do you actually think I had something to do with what happened to him?"

Smith had a strong feeling Louise Platt's father was telling the truth.

"We have to cover all angles, Mr Platt. Is Louise at home right now?"

Mr Platt pointed to the ceiling. "Do you think I like to listen to music like that? She's pretty much been holed up in her room since this morning when she found out what had happened to Ashe."

"How did she find out so soon?" Smith was shocked at how quickly the news had spread.

"Social Media, probably. You know how quickly things spread these days."

"We need to speak to Louise," Smith told him. "And as she's only fourteen it would be better if you're there when we do."

Mr Platt placed his hand on the chair arm and managed to prise himself out of the chair.

"It's such a curse carrying all this weight around," He said. "My father was seven-foot-two, so I suppose I can't complain too much. I'll see if I can persuade Louise to leave her room."

CHAPTER NINE

Whitton and Yang Chu had drawn a blank with Peter Ashe's wife. Heidi Ashe hadn't been able to tell them much more than she'd told Smith the day before. She maintained that the last time she spoke to her husband was on Thursday when she went to the house to collect some of her things. She hadn't seen him since then.

"Do you think she's telling the truth?" Yang Chu asked as they drove back towards the city.

"I believed her," Whitton said. "And I can't imagine her as the kind of woman who would chop off her husband's bits."

"Me neither," Yang Chu said and shivered. "What now?"

"Wait and see what else turns up. I'm sure my husband will have found out something from that schoolgirl."

"Do you think they're going to bring someone in to replace Brownhill?" Yang Chu changed the subject.

"Probably," Whitton sighed. "Some outsider who's first objective will be to shake things up and stamp their authority. Remember when Brownhill first arrived? It was a nightmare."

"Wasn't Smith offered the DI job?"

"He was, but he wasn't really in a good place at the time. He'd just lost everything – his house, his girlfriend and very nearly his sanity."

"Maybe they'll offer it to him again," Yang Chu suggested. "I mean, he never really took orders from Brownhill anyway did he? He could do the job in his sleep. Just think of the pay increase."

"Sadly, my husband doesn't care about money one little bit. It's just something that's there in the background in his eyes."

They parked in the car park at the station and got out of the car. The clear skies from earlier were beginning to cloud over and rain was definitely on the cards. They went inside and headed for Bridge's office. The room was deathly quiet and Bridge and PC Baldwin were staring at something on the screen of a laptop computer.

"Find anything?" Whitton asked.

Baldwin turned around. "Nothing at all. We've gone through the database and there's nothing like this on there. A woman was arrested for chopping off her husband's thingy in a fit of rage a while ago, but she soon calmed down and even had the presence of mind to put it in a bag and then in ice. They managed to sew it back on."

"Will you please stop calling it a thingy?" Bridge said. "That's just all wrong."

"We didn't get anything from the wife either," Yang Chu said. "She still claims she hadn't seen her husband since Thursday, and she can't think of anybody who would want to harm him."

"This really is a weird one," Whitton said. "No sign of a break in – this was definitely not a botched burglary, and why chop off his manhood?"

"And why stab him in the heart when he would have certainly died from the loss of blood in his nether regions anyway?" Yang Chu added.

"It looks like quite a party is going on in here," Smith appeared in the doorway.

"I'm afraid we've had a wasted few hours," Whitton told him. "Heidi Ashe couldn't give us anything more to go on, and Bridge and Baldwin drew a blank with the database too. Please tell me you've found something."

"No," Smith said.

"Then how do you explain that ridiculous smile on your face?"

"We didn't get much out of the schoolgirl," Smith said. "But Webber's on his way in for a briefing. It looks like he might have our first positive lead. He'll be here in about twenty minutes so I'm going up to the canteen to get a coffee before he arrives."

* * *

Half an hour later, the team gathered in the conference room, all eager to hear what the Head of Forensics had to tell them.

Webber opened up a folder and took out a printout. "I've found out about the knife that was sticking out of Peter Ashe's chest. It really is an unusual knife."

"How on earth did you find out what it is so quick?" Bridge asked.

"Google," Webber said and grinned. "I pasted a photo into the search bar and got the results straight away. It's called a Kila, and it's a three-sided peg knife. It has its origins in Tibet and it's primarily used as a ritual tool of the Buddhists."

"I don't mean to sound stupid," Smith said. "But I thought the Buddhists were totally against violence."

He glanced at Yang Chu.

"Why the hell are you looking at me?" The young DC said. "I'm third generation Vietnamese – I'm more of a Yorkshireman than you'll ever be, and what I know about Buddhism could be written on a postage stamp."

"Calm down," Smith said. "We know that Buddhism is a non-violent religion, all I'm wondering is why was a Buddhist knife used here?"

"That's true," Webber said. "I don't know an awful lot about Buddhism, but I'm just giving you what I found out about this particular knife. Traditionally its purpose is as a ritual implement, which a shaman would use to harmonise the ground during ceremonies. The blade would be thrust into the ground and ensure the stability essential for prayer."

"That's all very well," Smith said. "But how is that relevant in this instance? Why stab a man with a knife usually used in prayer?"

"That's just one of the ways a Kila was used," Webber continued. "It was also used as a tool of exorcism."

"Exorcism?" Whitton exclaimed.

"Exorcism," Webber repeated. "The Buddhists believed that the Kila could hold negative energies in place. Once the demons had been expelled from their human hosts, this knife acted as a kind of permanent holding cell for the demons after purification."

Smith shot up in his chair so suddenly that everybody turned to stare at him.

"Say that part again," he said to Webber.

"The Kila acted as a kind of permanent holding cell," Webber said. "It's a crude analogy but it fits."

"You mentioned demons," Smith raised his voice. "Peter Ashe received a message on his phone at 8pm on Friday. It mentioned something about demons. We need to have a closer look at that phone – I've got a feeling that Mr Ashe was already dead when the message was sent, and I also believe whoever sent the message is the same person that killed him."

CHAPTER TEN

Have you had a chance to think about what we talked about earlier?"
Chalmers asked Smith in the car park at the station.

They were both standing outside, smoking cigarettes. Webber had called one of his technicians and explained that Peter Ashe's phone log was their main priority and they were waiting for some news.

"Give me a chance, boss," Smith said, exhaling a cloud of smoke. "This recent murder has occupied all of my thoughts. I told you, I'll think about it."

"Well don't take too long. The post won't stay open forever you know."

"I told you," Smith said. "I'll give it some thought."

"Give what some thought?" Whitton had come outside without Smith noticing.

"Your husband here has been offered the DI job on a silver plate and he needs some time to think about it," Chalmers told her.

Smith could feel his face warming up.

Whitton glared at him. "You didn't tell me about this."

"Firstly," Smith took a long drag of his cigarette to give him time to think of what to say. "I haven't officially been offered the DI gig, and, secondly, I only found out about it an hour or so ago. Can you two please just get off my back?"

He threw the cigarette butt into the distance, scowled at Chalmers and went back inside the station.

"I hope I haven't caused any shit," Chalmers said. "Strictly speaking, what Smith said is true. The post hasn't been officially advertised yet – I heard about it through the grapevine, and I only put the idea in his head a short while ago. Don't give him grief over it. You know Smith – he won't do anything he doesn't want to do."

"He'd better accept that job," Whitton said. "I have to get back in – Webber's technician has found something about the message on Paul Ashe's phone."

"We now know two things," Grant Webber began.

The Head of Forensics had a pile of papers in front of him.

"Kenny Bean has narrowed down Paul Ashe's time of death to a window of an hour and a half. He died between six and seven-thirty on Friday evening. Cause of death was blood loss from the amputated penis. It appears the knife to the heart was merely an afterthought. The second thing we now know is the phone message he received that evening was sent when he was already dead. It was sent at eight on the dot."

"Can we trace the sender?" Smith said.

"That's going to take some time," Webber told him.

"What about the two phone calls earlier that day?" Smith remembered. "Same number?"

"That we do know. Harry, my technician simply called the number from his own phone. It was Heidi Ashe, Peter's wife. She confirmed that she phoned her husband twice that afternoon. The first call wasn't answered but she got through on the second attempt. She merely wanted to remind him she was coming round to fetch some more of her belongings the following day."

"So, we really won't know anything more until we can trace the owner of the phone who left that message," Bridge pointed out. "What did it say in the message again?"

Webber rifled through the papers in front of him. "*God has forgiven you your sins. But He could not rid you of your demons, so I've taken them for you.*"

"What does that even mean?" Bridge asked.

"I think it means we have a real sicko on our hands," Smith said. "With what we now know about the knife, it seems to me we have an individual who believes he is some kind of God."

"I don't get it," Bridge said.

"God has forgiven you your sins," Smith quoted the message. "I've taken your demons. Come on, Bridge, this is the work of someone playing the role of God."

The room was silent. Nobody seemed to know what to say next.

"Where do you suggest we look next then?" Bridge addressed the question to nobody in particular.

"Religion," Chalmers said.

"Religion?" Bridge repeated.

"If our killer is on some kind of God trip, he may have had a run in with the church."

"I agree," Smith joined in. "One way to interpret the message is the sender has no faith in God's power anymore, so he's taken on the job that God wasn't able to do. And that could mean he's been let down by the church somehow."

"That's a bit far-fetched isn't it?" Whitton said.

"Do you have any better interpretations?" Smith said.

"I just think you might be making this a lot more complicated than it actually is. What if it's simply a case of somebody getting revenge on an adulterer?"

"A sick one at that," Bridge added. "He was sleeping with a schoolgirl remember."

Smith looked his wife in the eyes. "Have you not been paying attention? Peter Ashe had his penis chopped off. If that wasn't enough, someone decided to stick a knife in his heart. And not just any knife – it was a knife that's used in Buddhist rituals to capture demons. After his heart stopped beating, a message was sent from someone claiming to have taken his demons. This is not a simple case of anything, Whitton. I suggest you wake up a bit and listen to what's being said."

Everybody in the room looked at him. Whitton opened her mouth to speak then closed it again. She glared at her husband, stood up and left the room.

"That was uncalled for," Chalmers told Smith. "Totally uncalled for."

"You're sleeping on the sofa tonight, mate," Bridge chipped in.

"Let's recap from the very beginning," Smith ignored them both.

"I think we've exhausted all avenues for today," Chalmers said with authority in his voice. "It's getting late and going over it all again isn't going to help right now. We'll start again early tomorrow with fresh heads and hopefully fresh ideas."

Nobody had any arguments. The sound of scraping chairs was heard and everybody except Smith and Chalmers left the conference room.

"What the hell is wrong with you?" Chalmers demanded.

"I feel like I'm surrounded by idiots at times," Smith replied. "Why can't anybody else see that this murder isn't a simple revenge killing – it goes much deeper than that. There is something about the ritual knife and the odd message that is really important. Why am I the only one who can see that?"

"They're not idiots," Chalmers said. "You know very well they're not idiots. Unfortunately, you tend to operate on a totally different wavelength to everybody else sometimes. And that's what makes you a bloody good detective and a royal pain in the arse at the same time. Go home. Apologise to your wife. Whitton didn't deserve that, and you know it."

CHAPTER ELEVEN

Chalmers words wouldn't leave Smith's head during the drive home. He knew he could have worded what he said to Whitton in the conference room better, but his sentiments were the same. He meant what he said. The more he thought about it, the angrier he became.

Why the hell should I apologise to one of my team for telling them how to do their job properly? He thought.

The fact that Whitton was his wife was irrelevant. She had even insisted on more than one occasion that he treat her no differently than he would anyone else.

It was still light outside when Smith turned into his road. He still didn't know what he was going to say to Whitton when he got home. Maybe his words were a bit harsh, but Whitton's reaction was downright unprofessional. He got out of the car and walked up the path to the front door. Whitton's car was nowhere to be seen. He went inside and walked through to the kitchen to let the dogs in. Whitton and Laura weren't home. Theakston and Fred didn't even greet him when Smith opened the back door. They walked past him, obviously wondering where the other two humans were.

"I don't know where they are," Smith told them both.

He filled their bowls with food and went outside to the back garden. He lit a cigarette, took out his phone and dialled Whitton's number. It went straight to voicemail. Smith ended the call without leaving a message. He knew that Whitton was probably at her parents' house; they'd been looking after Laura, and Whitton was probably lingering there, calming down a bit.

Theakston finished his food first. The fat Bull Terrier came outside and gazed up at Smith, obviously looking for a refill. Fred, the repugnant Pug appeared to be savouring every mouthful. Smith finished the cigarette and went back inside. He tried phoning Whitton again with the same result.

"She's mad at me," he told Fred.

The ugly Pug was licking his lips in a gruesome way. The snorts and lip-slapping noises made Smith smile. The growling noise coming from Smith's stomach reminded him he hadn't eaten all day. He picked up his house keys and left the house. His phone was still on the kitchen table.

As he walked the mile or so to the Hog's Head, Smith went over the murder of Peter Ashe in his head. Ashe had died between six and seven-thirty on Friday evening. He was alone in the house because his wife was staying with her sister after finding out her husband was having an affair with a fourteen-year-old schoolgirl. Cause of death was loss of blood after having his penis hacked off. He was also stabbed in the heart with a knife normally used in Buddhist rituals to imprison demons. Ashe received a message on his phone claiming that the sender had done what God was unable to do.

"Why did you send the message after you'd already killed Peter Ashe?" Smith spoke out loud and an old lady walking her dog gave him a strange look.

"Evening," Smith said to her. "Lovely evening for a walk."

The old lady quickened her pace.

Smith walked past the park where he used to take the dogs for walks and made a mental note to do it again the next chance he got. Theakston in particular was bordering on obese.

Somebody knew about Peter Ashe's affair, he thought. And that's why he was killed in such a symbolic way.

Smith was convinced the schoolgirl's father had nothing to do with it, and he could also discount Ashe's wife. In any other apparent revenge-killing those two would be the prime suspects, but Smith was positive neither of them had anything to do with Peter Ashe's death.

Who does that leave, then?

He tried to push all the thoughts spinning around in his head aside when he went inside the Hog's Head. It was relatively busy for a Sunday evening. Marge, the owner of the pub was nowhere to be seen. Smith ordered a pint of Theakstons at the bar and took it outside to the beer garden.

"Jason," Marge was clearing glasses from a recently vacated table. "It's lovely to see you again."

"You too, Marge. It's nice and busy in there this evening."

"Spring is on the way," Marge said. "It seems to bring people out. Are you here on your own?"

"Whitton is at her parents'," Smith didn't feel like elaborating. "They've been looking after Laura. We were called into work this weekend."

"Nothing serious, I hope?"

"We're not sure yet. I'm starving. Do you still have the steak and ale pie on the menu?"

"It's one of our bestsellers. I'll put your order in."

"Thanks, Marge. I'll eat inside though – spring might be on the way but it's not quite shorts and T-Shirt weather just yet."

Smith lit a cigarette and took a big swig of beer. When he put the glass down he noticed he'd finished half of it in one go.

"Great minds think alike," Baldwin appeared next to him.

She was also holding a pint of beer.

"It's been a rough day," Smith said. "What brings you here?"

"I didn't feel like going home to an empty flat. I thought I'd put it off for a while."

"Have you eaten yet?"

"It's not much fun eating on your own," she sighed. "Although you'd have thought I'd have got used to it by now."

"I've just ordered a steak and ale pie," Smith told her. "Let's go inside and ask Marge to make that two."

They sat at a table close to the bar. Smith's usual table was occupied by a couple with a small boy aged around eight or nine. The child was sitting quietly reading a book. Smith watched him for a while and smiled. It was quite refreshing to see such a young boy sitting quite contentedly with a book in front of him. Smith was more used to children tearing around the room or obsessing over something on their mobile phones.

"Where's Whitton?" Baldwin broke Smith's reverie.

"At her parents' house I assume."

"You assume?"

"Your guess is as good as mine," Smith said and finished the beer in his glass. "I tried phoning but it went straight to voicemail."

"You were a bit rude to her in the briefing if you don't mind me saying."

"I don't get you lot," Smith said. "You women. You say one thing and mean something completely different. Whitton clearly stated that she expects no special favours from me at work. Those were her exact words. She said that just because we're married it doesn't mean I'm to treat her any differently to any other DC. I merely pointed out she needed to pay attention to what's really going on in this case. This isn't a revenge killing – this is something else altogether."

"I'm listening. What exactly do you think we're dealing with here?"

"Hold that thought," Smith stood up. "I'll get us some more drinks."

He returned with two fresh pints. "Where were we?"

"You were about to give me your professional opinion on why Peter Ashe had to die," Baldwin said with a wry smile.

Smith smiled back. Their eyes met for a moment, but Baldwin quickly broke eye contact. Smith could feel his face flush slightly – he felt something stir inside his stomach, and he took a sip of his beer to try and put what had just happened out of his mind. It didn't work. He had always found Baldwin attractive, but the feeling he'd just experienced was more than simple attraction.

Much, much more.

He drank some more beer and put his glass down. "Peter Ashe was cheating on his wife with a fourteen-year-old. In a normal investigation, the first person we would suspect would be his wife, especially as we know she knew about the affair. Second on the list would be the girl's father. Neither of them did this – that, I'm ninety-nine percent certain of."

"And who's next on the list of suspects?" Baldwin asked.

"In a normal investigation?"

"Right."

"Then we'd look more closely at Ashe himself. Did he have any enemies? Did he owe money to anybody? Was he hiding some secret that would explain why he was murdered?"

"And?"

"That's what my point was back in the briefing," Smith was becoming quite animated. "This *isn't* a normal investigation. The fact that his dick was cut off and he was stabbed in the heart with an unusual knife afterwards suggests this is far from a normal case. That's why I got a bit angry. Because I seem to be the only one who can see that this investigation is different. If we carry on investigating this the way we usually would – motive, victim, weapon etc, we are not going to get anywhere."

"I'm afraid you've lost me there," Baldwin admitted.

"What if the motive had nothing to do with the victim himself?"

"Now I'm really confused."

"We've been working on the assumption the killer did this to Peter Ashe. That it was personal. Forget Peter Ashe the man - concentrate on Peter Ashe the adulterer who had a thing for teenage girls."

"Are you saying it could have been anyone?" Baldwin said. "Do you think Peter Ashe was just unlucky? That he was just one of any number of perverts who could just have easily been chosen?"

"Bingo," Smith said so loudly that the young boy looked up from the book he was reading.

Smith raised his glass in the air. "Cheers, PC Baldwin. Finally, someone is on the same wavelength as me."

CHAPTER TWELVE

"Forgive me father for I have sinned."
The speaker on the table crackled and the man started to panic. With a practiced hand he smacked the top of the box it was contained in and the crackling noise stopped. He glanced at the screen on his phone – 21:25.
A confession under cover of darkness, he thought. *Father Swift is working late tonight.*
Night-time confessions always brought out the bleakest depths of the soul, and the ensuing demons were much easier to capture at night. When they felt most at ease.
In the inky black of night.
The man turned up the volume on the speaker and listened.

This confession was brief, but in the fleeting minutes between beginning and end the man knew.
He knew instinctively how these particular demons would be taken.
He gazed affectionately at the row of Kila's lined up against one wall and selected the most appropriate one for the occasion. An exquisite example of Tibetan workmanship. The three-edged knife had a handle constructed of hardwood. The carving on the wood represented the three poisons emerging from the head of the liturgal crocodile. The man ran the one-foot-long knife through his hands. It was warm to the touch.

The mobile phone on the table next to the speaker box started to ring. The man placed the Kila on the carpet and went to answer the phone. He listened as the voice on the other end gave him the information he needed. He ended the call without having spoken a single word.

He wrapped the selected Kila in a thin leather cloth and tucked it into his belt over his shirt. It would be concealed when he donned the black jacket that he always kept in his car. He would only put on the jacket at the last minute. He checked the shape of the black tie he was wearing, picked up his car keys and phone and went out into the night.

CHAPTER THIRTEEN

Smith and Baldwin ate their food without once mentioning the investigation. Baldwin finished first. "That was delicious. I can see why you always order that in here."

Smith's pie had him beaten. He placed his knife and fork on the plate next to the uneaten pastry crust.

"Either I wasn't as hungry as I thought," he said, wiping his mouth on a napkin. "Or Marge's portions have got bigger. It's been a while since I was here. Right, PC Baldwin, I'll organise us some more drinks and we can see how much more we can agree on tonight."

"I should be getting home," Baldwin told Smith when he came back from the bar.

"Back to your empty flat?" Smith said.

"What about Whitton? Shouldn't you try and get hold of her again?"

"I'll let her know where I am," Smith said. "But we're going to carry on where we left off before the pies arrived. We're both agreed on the reason why Peter Ashe was killed, right? It wasn't because of who he was but what he was. He had his thingy – as you quite beautifully put it, lopped off because he was cheating on his wife."

"Or because he fancied schoolgirls," Baldwin suggested.

"It doesn't matter," Smith said. "The point is we don't need to waste any more time looking into poor Mr Ashe."

Smith was feeling quite drunk. He'd lost count of how many beers he'd had since he arrived.

"So, where do you suggest we start looking?" he continued. "Bearing in mind the fact that Ashe himself isn't personally involved."

"People who dislike perverts?" Baldwin thought out loud.

"That narrows it down to most of the population."

"People who hate perverts who have also got their hands on Tibetan knives recently, then."

"And here's me thinking I was the only smart one on the team," Smith said. He tried to take a sip of beer but ended up with most of it running down his chin onto the table.

Baldwin started to laugh. It was an endearing laugh, and quite contagious. Smith followed suit. Their eyes met again, but this time Baldwin held Smith's gaze for much longer.

"You have really weird eyes," Smith said.

"Thanks a lot."

"I meant it in a nice way. They're very unusual."

"My mum used to say they changed colour depending on my moods," Baldwin told him.

Smith moved in closer. "Right now, they're dark green. What does that mean? What mood are you in now?"

"I think it's time to call it a night," Baldwin suggested. "I think you need some sleep and you should definitely find out where Whitton is."

"I'll call her," Smith searched inside his pockets for his phone, but he couldn't find it. "I must have left my phone at home. Whitton will be fine."

"It's getting late," Baldwin said, but her eyes were still smiling.

"We're on a roll," Smith insisted. "Your brain is on a roll. Go on."

"If we look at the murder from this new perspective, we still need to ask ourselves a few questions."

"Good."

"Why is this person killing perverts?" Baldwin said. "How is he finding out this information about the victim, and how does he manage to put his plan into action?"

"Why, how and how?" Smith said and grinned.

"Sorry?"

"Why?" Smith said. "Because, according to the message he sent afterwards, he believes God is not doing His job. How he found out about the victim is still unknown to us, as is how he managed to gain access to Mr Ashe's house. I need a pee."

He stood up and swaggered towards the toilets.

Baldwin was standing up when Smith returned. "I really have to get going. Thanks for the company."

"No," Smith said. "No, no, no. Thank you."

"I'll see you at work tomorrow."

"I'll walk you home," Smith offered.

"There's no need."

"What! Let a young woman walk home on her own through the violence and evil of the city? I wouldn't hear of it. Besides, it's only a short distance from my house."

Baldwin laughed again. "If you insist."

Smith managed to light a cigarette on the third attempt and inhaled deeply. The combination of the sudden rush of nicotine and the alcohol consumed that evening made him feel very light-headed. His vision turned black for a few seconds then returned.

"Are you alright?" Baldwin asked.

"Temporary blackout," Smith said. "Happens all the time. Coffee helps."

"Make sure you get some coffee inside you soon then," Baldwin laughed.

They carried on walking in silence.

"This is me," Baldwin stopped outside her flat. "Thank you for tonight. And thanks for walking me home."

"It was my pleasure," Smith said and grimaced.

"Are you sure you're alright?"

"I need coffee," Smith told her. "Right now."

Baldwin's flat was just as Smith had expected it to be. Everything seemed to have its place. The kitchen tops were spotless and there wasn't a speck of dust to be seen. Smith slumped down on one of the chairs next to the kitchen table while Baldwin made the coffee.

"Do you realise," Smith said. "We've worked together for all these years and this is the first time I've been inside your flat."

Baldwin spooned some coffee in two cups and filled them with hot water. Sirens could be heard in the distance. Police sirens if Smith wasn't mistaken.

"Well?" he said.

"I didn't realise you had asked a question," Baldwin said and put the coffee cups on the table.

The sirens were getting closer. An ambulance had now joined in.

"You sounded just like me for a second then." Smith said.

"You must be a bad influence," Baldwin said and sat down next to him.

Smith sipped the coffee. It was strong with no sugar. "That's better. I'll be fine in a minute."

"I wonder what all the noise is about," Baldwin had heard the sirens too.

"Not our problem," Smith said. "For one night they can be somebody else's problem. Can I ask you something?"

"Of course."

"It's a bit personal."

"Shoot."

"How come you still live on your own?"

Baldwin turned to face him. "What do you mean?"

Smith could now smell her perfume. "I mean you're quite a catch. You have a good job, you're a hell of a lot of fun to be around, and you're one of the most beautiful women I've ever met. I mean, those eyes…"

"And what are my eyes telling you now?" Baldwin said and moved closer.

Smith did the same. "I'm not quite sure. They appear to be slightly lighter green than they were earlier. What does that mean?"

He moved closer still so that their noses were almost touching. They were so close now Smith couldn't make out the colour of Baldwin's eyes. It didn't matter because they were no longer open. Smith kissed her gently on the lips. He placed his hand on the back of her neck and her lips opened over his. He closed his eyes and felt himself being washed away on a wave he had no control over.

CHAPTER FOURTEEN

It was not yet light when Smith left Baldwin's flat and started to walk home. His head was throbbing. He lit a cigarette and inhaled deeply. The sudden rush of nicotine made his vision turn black for a few moments, but when it returned Smith remembered all too clearly what had happened between him and Baldwin.

It made him feel sick.

He'd never done anything like that before and it disgusted him. He didn't even know where it had all started – one minute he was drinking coffee with a work colleague, and the next thing he knew he was waking up naked in bed beside her.

What have I done? he thought. *What the hell have I done?*

He reached his house and walked up the driveway. Whitton's car wasn't parked in its usual place, and for a moment Smith felt some relief. At least he wouldn't have to explain where he'd been until now if she was still with her parents. The relief didn't last long when flashes of the previous night came into his head. He still couldn't understand how it had happened. He was drunk, but he'd been drunk in the past and nothing like that had ever happened before.

He went inside the house and headed for the kitchen to make some coffee. Theakston and Fred were asleep on their beds on the floor. Neither of them even bothered to get up to greet him. It was as though they knew what Smith had done. He boiled the kettle and glanced at the phone on the kitchen table. The screen was flashing. He picked it up and saw he'd received forty-five messages and missed twenty-six calls.

Something was seriously wrong.

He opened up the first message. It was from Yang Chu telling him to phone back immediately. Smith read a further five messages, they were all similar to Yang Chu's. He'd missed calls from Yang Chu, Bridge, Chalmers and Grant Webber. Whitton's mum and dad had also tried to get hold of him.

Smith dialled Yang Chu's number and it was answered straight away.

"Where the hell have you been, Sarge? We've been trying to get hold of you all night."

"Battery died," Smith lied. "What's the urgency?"

"Whitton was involved in a car accident yesterday evening," Yang Chu told him. "She was driving home from her parents' house when a car pulled out in front of her without looking. Whitton drove straight into him."

"Of my God," Smith said. "Is she going to be alright?"

A thought suddenly struck him and he felt his stomach warming up.

"If she was driving home she will have had Laura in the car with her."

"Calm down," Yang Chu said. "Laura was strapped in her seat in the back. She didn't have a scratch on her."

"Is Whitton going to be alright?" Smith asked again.

"They're not sure. She was wearing her seatbelt but it was quite an impact. Where were you?"

"I told you," Smith said. "The battery on my phone died. It happens, Yang Chu."

"You weren't at home, Sarge. I came round to tell you but there was nobody home."

"It's not important," Smith said. "I'll get to the hospital as soon as I can."

Smith had a quick shower. He knew he should really drive straight to the hospital, but he was sure he could still smell Baldwin's perfume on him. It was a sweet, heavy smell. Last night the aroma had intoxicated him, but right now the lingering scent made him feel sick to the stomach. He stood under the hot jets of water and closed his eyes. He scrubbed and scrubbed until he was certain that all traces of Baldwin were gone, but it didn't help. It didn't alter the fact that while his wife and daughter were being driven off in an ambulance he was enjoying the warmth of another woman. He turned off the shower, dried and got dressed quickly. All traces of Baldwin were now gone, but Smith knew that wasn't going to be enough.

* * *

He found the doctor who was treating Whitton by the front desk. He was a doctor Smith had never met before. He was talking to Whitton's dad, Harold.

"I came as soon as I heard," Smith told Harold. "Are they going to be alright?"

"Dr Lowell," the doctor introduced himself. "It appears the car your wife was driving had a rather nasty crash. Your wife was found unconscious at the scene and her condition hasn't changed. She's been stabilised, and we'll have a better understanding of how serious her injuries are when we've finished all the tests."

"What about Laura? The little girl who was in the car with her?"

"She's going to be fine," Dr Lowell said. "She's awake and she's managed to eat something. Quite a bit as a matter of fact."

"That sounds like Laura." A smile appeared on Smith's face.

Then he felt the smile fade. It was replaced with a quivering sensation on his top lip and followed by a numbness that spread from his chin to his eyes. Then the tears came.

The tears came quickly. Smith wiped his eyes, but it didn't seem to help. Harold Whitton placed his hand on Smith's shoulder. "Get a grip, son. You're no use to anyone in this condition."

"Sorry," Smith blubbered. "I'm so sorry."

"Your wife and child don't need you to be sorry, son," Harold said. "They need you to be strong."

This seemed to do the trick. The tears stopped. Smith wiped his face and took a few deep breaths.

"Can I see her?" he asked Dr Lowell. "Can I see my wife?"

"She's undergoing a CT scan right now," Dr Lowell told him. "We'll keep you informed of what's going on. I'm sure your daughter would love to see you, though. Mr Whitton can show you where she is."

Laura was sitting up in bed when Smith and Harold Whitton came into the ward. Jane, Whitton's mum was sitting on a chair next to her.

"Hello, love," Jane said to Smith. "She's going to be fine. She hasn't stopped eating since she came in." She turned to Harold. "Any news about Erica?"

"They're still busy with tests," Harold told her. "The doctor said he'll keep us up to date. She's a tough one and I'm sure she'll be fine."

"Hey, my beautiful girl," Smith leaned over and kissed Laura on the top of the head.

He couldn't see a scratch on her. There was no indication that she'd been in a car crash whatsoever.

"Your mum's going to be fine and ordering us around again in no time," Smith told her.

"They reckon things could have been much different if she wasn't strapped into her seat," Jane said. "That thing probably saved her life."

"When can she come home?"

"They're going to keep her in overnight, just as a precaution. She might have a delayed concussion or whiplash, although they said that's probably unlikely."

"It was Erica who took the brunt," Harold said. "The police say the idiot just pulled out right in front of her without looking. Bastard walked away from the crash with a couple of bruises. Can I have a word?"

"Of course."

"Let's get a cup of coffee," Harold suggested. "It tastes like dishwater but it's better than nowt."

"Where were you?" Harold Whitton came straight to the point.

He and Smith sat opposite one another in one of the hospital canteens.

"What do you mean?" Smith said.

"I mean what I said. Where were you? We couldn't get hold of you."

Smith really didn't want to lie to his father-in-law, but he didn't see any other option.

"The battery on my phone died," he gave him the same story he'd given Yang Chu.

"I came to the house, son," Harold said. "You weren't home."

"I had something to eat at the Hog's Head." At least that part was true.

"I knocked on your door at half-two in the morning," Harold told him. "All the lights were off inside the house and your car wasn't there."

Harold looked him directly in the eye and Smith could feel his face burning.

"Where were you?" Harold asked again.

Making the biggest mistake of my life, Smith thought.

He really didn't know what to say. Harold Whitton was no fool and Smith knew he would see straight through any lie Smith told him.

"Mrs Whitton said I'd find you in here," Dr Lowell had come into the canteen. "We've finished with the CT scan and it appears to be all clear. And Erica woke up just after we'd finished. She complained about how cold it was inside the machine. I've got a feeling she's going to be just fine."

Smith breathed in deeply. He could feel Harold Whitton's eyes on him, and he knew Harold was not going to let the matter of Smith's whereabouts drop.

CHAPTER FIFTEEN

Whitton was lying with her eyes closed. A drip was feeding something into a vein in her arm and there was a screen next to the bed monitoring her vitals. Smith sat down next to her and held her hand. She opened her eyes and looked up at him.

"The doctor told me Laura is going to be fine," she croaked.

"That's right," Smith squeezed her hand. "Although I think the hospital is going to run out of food if she stays in much longer. How are you feeling?"

"Like I've been hit by a bus. Everything hurts. What happened?"

"Don't you remember?"

"I remember bits," Whitton said and winced. "I remember driving back home – we'd just got off the ring road and then there was a bang and I woke up in here. Everything else is a bit of a blur."

At that moment Smith realised something that made him shiver. He realised how life can change in a fraction of a second. If the driver of the other car had bothered to look before pulling into the road, Whitton wouldn't have crashed into him and she would have been at home when he got back from work. He wouldn't have gone to the Hog's Head, and he wouldn't have bumped into Baldwin there.

Everything would have worked out very differently. Everything would be OK.

His phone started to ring in his pocket. He ignored it.

"Answer it," Whitton said. "It could be work, and I feel really tired. I need to get some sleep."

Smith let go of her hand and stood up and answered the phone.

"Sarge." It was Yang Chu.

"What's wrong?" Smith said.

"We've had a call come in. A woman was babbling about finding her son covered in blood."

"Was he in a fight?"

"She found him on the carpet in the bedsit he rents," Yang Chu said. "Me and Bridge have just arrived. It looks like he's been murdered."

"I'll be there as soon as I can."

"There's more, Sarge. His hands have been chopped off and there's a knife sticking out of his chest."

* * *

The address Yang Chu gave Smith was in one of the less desirable parts of town. Tang Hall had a reputation for being *the* place to avoid in York, especially at night. Gangs of youths with nothing better to do roamed the streets, and violence was commonplace. Smith got out of the car and made sure to lock the doors. Even though there were already three police cars outside the house that meant nothing in Tang Hall.

A small crowd of onlookers had already gathered around the police cars. Two girls with grubby toddlers in pushchairs were trying to look inside the house.

"What's going on?" one of them asked.

She couldn't have been much older than sixteen.

"None of your business," Smith told her. "Haven't you got something better to do? Like giving your baby a bath?"

"Knob-end," the young mother said and walked away up the road.

"Charming," a middle-aged PC had heard her. "I don't know what's wrong with kids these days. Tang Hall has always produced its fair share of scrotes, but this lot are just out of control."

Smith walked past him towards the house. Bridge was standing in the doorway.

"Morning," he said. "How's Whitton doing?"

"She's going to be fine. What have we got?"

"John Ware. Twenty-two-years old. Looks like the same killer as the other one," Bridge told him. "His hands were chopped off and the knife sticking out of his chest is similar to the one Peter Ashe had stuck in his heart."

"Where is he?"

"Second door on the right. Dr Bean is already inside. Webber's just got here, too."

The plaque on the wall next to the front door read *Willow Heights*. Smith thought that whoever came up with that name must have had some kind of warped sense of humour. The building was a Victorian three-storey affair that had been converted into individual bedsits. There were examples of similar buildings all around York. Greedy landlords had cottoned on to the idea that the more tenants you could cram inside, the more money there was to be made. And, as the people who lived in places like these were mostly second, sometimes third-generation benefits recipients, the landlords received their rent directly from the government.

Willow Heights was in a sad state of disrepair. Cracks ran down the walls and in some places gaping holes were visible where huge chunks of plaster had fallen away. Inside the door was a rusty bicycle that had obviously not been used for quite some time. One of the wheels had been removed, and the other tyre was totally flat. There was a musty smell inside – it smelled like carpet that hadn't been cleaned for quite some time. Smith stopped in the doorway and looked inside the room. Grant Webber was examining something on a table on the far side by the window. Dr Kenny Bean was leaning over what Smith assumed to be John Ware.

"Morning Webber," Smith said. "OK if I come in? I won't touch anything."

"How's Whitton doing?" The Head of Forensics asked without looking up.

"She's going to be fine. Morning, Kenny. Found anything?"

"I've only just arrived," Dr Bean straightened up. "He's definitely dead. I can tell you that much."

"This place isn't exactly a palace is it?" Smith observed.

The room consisted of a bed that appeared to double up as a lounge suite. A shelf opposite held nothing more than a tiny microwave, an electric toaster and a kettle on it. Next to it was a small sink with a single tap.

"I don't know how people can live like this," Smith added.

"The forgotten generation," Webber said. "Only now it's more like generations. And the gap between those generations is getting shorter and shorter every year."

"I saw that outside," Smith said.

"This country has gone to the dogs," Webber growled. "They think they can shut these people away in places like this, pay their rent for them and forget all about them. There's no hope for this lot. Gone to the dogs I tell you."

"You're in a good mood this morning," Smith said. "Now, can you spare me the social commentary and tell me what we've got?"

"What we've got is a forensic nightmare," Webber said. "That's what we've got. If I were to hazard a guess I'd say the place hasn't been cleaned properly in months. If ever, which means there's going to be fingerprints and DNA in here dating back to the turn of the century."

Smith wasn't in the mood to press further. He turned his attention to the dead body next to the bed. "What do you think killed him?" He asked Dr Bean. "Initial thoughts?"

"Both hands were amputated," Dr Bean replied. "And from the amount of blood on the carpet in their vicinity, I'd say that's what he died from. I did spot something interesting straight away though."

"Go on."

"If you look at the blood on the carpet, you'll see it has spattered in all directions. North, east, south and west as it were."

"What does that tell us?"

"If this poor man was where he is now when his hands were cut off, the blood would initially spurt out but the main flow would be in one direction." He indicated this with a sweep of his hand. "It would have spurted that way and that way only."

"He was standing up when his hands were chopped off?" Smith speculated.

"It looks like it," Dr Bean said. "And we'll be able to confirm it when Mr Webber there has finished pontificating over the social ills of this once-great land and gets around to examining the spatters in detail."

"Where are the hands?" Smith asked nobody in particular.

"Gone," Webber answered. "Looks like whoever lopped them off took them with him."

"Did you ever find Peter Ashe's member at the other crime scene?"

"No, we didn't."

"What the hell is going on here?" Smith said. "First a poor man has his whip hacked off and now Mr Ware here is missing a pair of hands. Who would chop them off and take them with him?"

Webber looked at him. "You know my reply to that already."

"That's my department. Why do I always get the hard jobs? Maybe I ought to put in a transfer to forensics."

"Over my dead body," Webber said.

"Did you find a mobile phone?" Smith asked.

"Not yet. I got here five minutes before you, and if you don't mind, I'd appreciate it if you would piss off and leave me to do my job."

Smith couldn't resist it. "You'll let me know if you find anything?"

He was out of the door before Webber had time to reply.

CHAPTER SIXTEEN

The murder of John Ware had side-tracked Smith from the guilt that had been burning away inside him earlier, but as he drove away from the Tang Hall Estate, the sickening feeling returned in his stomach once more. He wasn't sure what to do. He'd never lied to Whitton before and he wasn't sure if he would be able to keep a secret like this bottled up for too long before it started to eat him away inside.

"Put it out of your mind," he told his reflection in the rear-view mirror. "It's going to have to wait until this investigation is over."

He thought about something else. He thought about the two recent murders. Peter Ashe and John Ware. Both were men in their twenties – both of them had body parts removed and both were stabbed in the heart with unusual knives. They were both already dead when they were stabbed. Smith knew they had to look into any connections between the two men, but he had a feeling that wasn't important. There was some other reason they were targeted that had nothing to do with them being acquainted.

Any hopes of putting what had happened the night before behind him were dashed as soon as Smith walked inside the station. Baldwin was manning the front desk. Smith couldn't even make eye contact with her – he simply walked straight past and made his way up to the canteen. Chalmers was sitting alone by the window. The DCI appeared to be deep in thought. Smith got some coffee from the machine and sat down without Chalmers even realising.

"Morning, boss," he said. "Are you alright?"

"Fine," he said. "I didn't hear you come in."

"Are you sure you're alright?"

"I didn't sleep much last night. I don't know why – I've been working all weekend, and I thought I'd be buggered. I heard about the murder on the Tang Hall Estate. I believe it's not just a typical Tang Hall killing."

"Definitely not. Same MO as the one a couple of days ago. Bloke had his hands chopped off and then he was stabbed in the heart with the same kind of knife."

"Any leads?"

"Webber's still working on it. I'm actually a bit worried about him. He's not himself."

"It's only been a few weeks," Chalmers said. "He was advised to take more time off, but he didn't. He'll work it out in his own time. I assume you've called some kind of briefing this morning."

"I didn't think there was much point until Webber and Kenny Bean have some initials for us."

"What about the victim?" Chalmers said. "The one with no hands?"

"John Ware. Twenty-two-years old. That's all we know so far."

"Don't you think it might be pertinent to find out more?"

"I don't think it's relevant right now."

"Have you been smoking something?" Chalmers asked. "What happened to that old Smith thing where motive is everything?"

"This one feels different, boss."

"I've heard that before. Have you given any more thought to the DI position?"

"I've had a lot on my mind," Smith said.

"It's not going to wait for you, you know. Top brass couldn't give a monkey's arse about who fills the position as long as it's filled. Don't take too long. I'm late for a meeting with the Super. Do yourself a favour and find out more about this dead Tang Hall bloke. Have you even bothered with the other people in the building? Friends and the like?"

"Bridge and Yang Chu are on it, boss."

"Is there something going on I ought to know about?"

"Whitton's car crash shook me up a bit that's all," Smith said.

"Bollocks. I know you, Smith. There's something else. Your mind is somewhere else completely. You haven't even bothered with standard protocol. Normally by now you'd have a list of potential witnesses as long as your arm. Go back to the Tang Hall and do your bloody job."

"I told you – I don't think we'll get anything useful," Smith insisted.

"That was an order. In case you've forgotten I'm your DCI."

"We're a bit short-staffed right now," Smith wasn't giving up.

"Let me put this another way," Chalmers had raised his voice. "If word gets to the Super that we're not putting the usual effort into a stiff on the Tang Hall, it's my balls that are going to be on the chopping block. And I *will* make that your problem, you mark my words. And if the press gets so much of a gnat's fart about this, they're going to take us to the cleaners. Police nonchalance rife on low-income estate. I can just see the headlines now. Tang Hall is political, and top brass are going to want to see that we're pulling out all the stops."

"I don't follow politics, boss. Never been interested."

"Get there now. If you're short-staffed, take Baldwin with you. Go and do what they pay you to do. Now I'm really late for that meeting with the Super."

Smith closed the door of his office behind him and sat down at his desk. He took out his phone and called Harold Whitton.

"Hello," Harold answered it. "Harold here."

"Harold," Smith said. "It's me. Is there any news? How's Erica doing?"

"She's much better. She's got a cracked elbow where she hit it on the dash, and they suspect whiplash, but they've given her something for it."

"Do we know when she can come home?"

"It'll be another few days at least. But at least she's on the mend. It could've been a lot worse. Where are you?"

"At work," Smith told him. "There's been a murder on the Tang Hall Estate."

"I wouldn't even bother looking into it. Tang Hall looks after Tang Hall."

"I'll call again later," Smith said and rang off.

CHAPTER SEVENTEEN

Baldwin was speaking to someone on the phone when Smith approached the front desk. He waited for her to finish.

"I've got a job for you," Smith said. "Chalmers wants us to go to Tang Hall to help Bridge and Yang Chu out."

"I'm supposed to be looking after the front desk," Baldwin told him. Neither of them made eye contact.

"Go and find somebody to take over. Just do it."

Baldwin walked past him and returned a short while later with a young PC.

"That wasn't so hard was it?" Smith said. "Let's go."

Neither of them spoke for the first mile or so. Smith glanced at the speedometer and realised he was driving much faster than he normally did. He eased his foot off the accelerator. "We need to talk."

He slowed down even more and stopped next to an off licence.

"I'm sorry," he said. "What happened last night shouldn't have happened and I'm sorry."

"I was there too remember," Baldwin reminded him. "It wasn't a one-sided thing."

"What are we going to do about it?"

"What do you mean?"

"I need to tell Whitton," Smith said.

"What good will that do? What happened last night happened. End of story. What will you achieve by bringing it out in the open?"

"Whitton deserves to know the truth."

"And do you think the truth is going to make her feel better?" Baldwin said. "Do you really think the truth is going to make anyone feel better?"

"It can't make me feel any worse than I feel right now," Smith said. "You and me were in bed together while my wife and child were being taken to hospital. Either one of them could have been killed in that crash."

"But they weren't. They're both going to be OK. We're all going to be OK."

"So, you're saying we should keep this between us?" Smith said.

"Yes. These things happen all the time – lives shouldn't have to be ruined because two people made a mistake."

Smith didn't say anything else. He started the car and pulled away from the kerb. What Baldwin had suggested made logical sense, but he wasn't sure if his conscience would be able to agree with his logic on this one.

The scene at the Tang Hall house where John Ware was found dead hadn't changed. Three police cars were still parked outside, as were the cars belonging to Yang Chu, Grant Webber and Dr Kenny Bean. Smith and Baldwin got out of the car.

"I was almost attacked walking the beat just up the road from here," Baldwin said. "Even though we were in uniform it didn't mean anything to these people. I hate this place."

"Let's go and see if the residents of *Willow Heights* will talk to us, shall we?" Smith said and headed for the front door.

Webber and Dr Bean were just finishing off inside John Ware's bedsit.

"An ambulance is on the way," Dr Bean told Smith.

"Do you have anything else for us?" Smith asked him.

"I prefer to do my work in the comfort of my mortuary, but there was something I observed. The amputations were clean – surgical even, and whoever did this certainly knew where to cut, not only to ensure maximum blood loss, but to avoid the harder bones. They managed to bypass the Ulna yet still sever the Radial Artery, and I can tell you that is a very tricky thing to do."

"So, we're looking at somebody familiar with the human anatomy?"

"That would be my initial assessment. Now, if I'm not mistaken that great, hulking white thing outside is an ambulance. I'll be in touch when I'm finished."

Bridge and Yang Chu appeared in the doorway. Both of them looked exhausted.

"Thanks a lot," Bridge spoke to Smith directly. "Thanks for leaving us to deal with the pond-life in this building."

"Sorry," Smith said. "I had other things on my mind. Do I need to ask if you found anything?"

"What do you think, Sarge," Yang Chu said. "This lot wouldn't tell us if they'd taken a photograph of a murder in progress. They don't like us, and they certainly don't trust us."

"What about friends of John Ware?"

"Nobody wanted to tell us anything. It was a total waste of time."

"Where is his mother now?" Smith asked. "She's the one who found him isn't she?"

"That's right," Bridge said. "She's still at the hospital. She was in a bit of a state so they gave her a sedative and admitted her overnight. But I doubt she'll be in much of a state to talk."

"I'll see if I can have a word with her when I go and see Whitton later."

"How's she doing?"

"She's off the danger list. Whiplash, bruises and a cracked elbow. She was lucky she was wearing her seatbelt. Laura is acting like nothing even happened. All she seems to be concerned about is getting enough food inside her."

Webber finished packing his equipment and joined them in the hallway. He was holding something in his left hand.

"Is that Ware's mobile phone?" Smith pointed to it.

"It was in his bedsit," Webber said. "So I assume it's his."

"Have you checked the call log?"

"I'll do it back at the lab."

"Do it now."

"Excuse me?" Webber's eyes opened slightly wider. "Are you suddenly my boss?"

"Please, Webber. You're the one with the gloves on. Just check to see if there are any recent messages."

Webber sighed, but he humoured Smith. He took the phone out of the evidence bag, laid the bag on his case and placed the phone on top."

"It's an old phone. No fingerprint reader. And no password. There are two unread messages."

"Open them."

Webber did as he was asked. Smith watched as he read the words on the screen. "The first one is from his mother. Telling him she'll be popping round today. Well I'll be damned."

"What?" Smith said.

"The second message." Webber said and read it out.

"God has forgiven you your sins. But He could not rid you of your demons, so I've taken them for you."

CHAPTER EIGHTEEN

"Same message as the one we found on Peter Ashe's phone," Smith began the briefing. "Is there anyone who doesn't agree that we're looking at the same killer here?"

The small conference room was silent.

Bridge, Yang Chu and Baldwin waited for Smith to continue.

"I'm going to speak to John Ware's mother at the hospital later," he said. "She was the one who found him. As expected, the residents of the Tang Hall Estate are keeping their mouths shut, but Ware's mother might have something to tell us."

"What do you think we're looking at here, Sarge?" Yang Chu asked. "Some religious nutcase?"

"I have to admit that I really don't know. We've got two dead men, both of whom had parts of their body removed and both of whom were sent messages after they were killed."

"I don't understand that part," Bridge said. "Why would the killer send the messages after he's killed them? What's the point in that?"

"Calling card?" Baldwin suggested.

Everybody looked at her.

"Go on," Smith urged.

"I'm not suggesting we're dealing with a serial killer here," Baldwin continued. "But in many documented cases of serial killings, a calling card was left at the crime. A way for the murderer to own what he's done. Maybe this is merely this man's calling card. It is the digital age after all."

"Have we found the owner of the phone that sent the messages?" Yang Chu asked.

"No," Smith suddenly felt very stupid. "Webber's guy was supposed to be working on it. We need to speed him up a bit. Baldwin, you suggested something we also need to look into. The Kila knife. The Buddhist sacrificial knife. We need to find out where someone can get their hands on such a knife. We've got two now – one from Peter Ashe and one from John Ware, so we know the killer bought more than one. Where did he get them from?"

DCI Chalmers came in. "Sorry I'm late. What have I missed?"

Smith updated him.

"Right," Chalmers said. "As far as I see it, what we have so far is a bit of a balls-up."

"Boss?" Smith couldn't believe what he'd just heard.

"I look at the people in this room and do you know what I see?" Chalmers said.

"The suspense is killing us," Smith said.

"I see a bunch of trainee policemen and women, that's what I see. You are a team of experienced detectives, not a load of wet-behind-the-ear rookies straight out of training. It's time you started acting like detectives. I realise with Brownhill no longer with us the dynamic of the team has changed dramatically, but you need to change with it."

"What are you suggesting, boss?" Smith asked.

"Start again. It's as simple as that. You need to wipe the slate clean and start this investigation from scratch. It's all over the bloody place. Don't assume because it's an unusual case that it won't be cracked in the conventional way. Murder is not normal – it is not a rational act, and all murders are different, but the way we solve them very rarely changes. Start again the way you always have done before and you'll get there."

Nice speech boss, Smith thought, but didn't dare say it out loud.

He knew deep down that the DCI was right.

He stood up and walked up to the whiteboard on the wall. The ghosts of past investigations were still visible as faded scribbles on the boards. Smith remembered every single one of them. All of them different from the last, but all of them had been brought to their rightful conclusion in the same way. He picked up a marker pen.

"Peter Ashe," Smith wrote in bold letters on the left-hand side of the board. "Twenty-nine-years old, reasonably comfortably off. Lived in a nice estate. Killed at home. Cause of death was massive blood loss after his penis was amputated. Nothing at the scene to suggest any kind of struggle took place. He was stabbed in the heart with a Buddhist ritual knife after he died."

He stopped and thought for a second then started to write.

'*God has forgiven you your sins. But He could not rid you of your demons, so I've taken them for you.*'

"This message was left on his phone after he was killed."

After a few seconds, Smith wrote 'drugs' on the board and looked at the team. "Kenny Bean is still busy with the tox report so we'll know more when he's finished, but how did someone manage to chop off Mr Ashe's penis without him putting up any kind of struggle?"

"He had to be drugged first," Yang Chu agreed.

"John Ware," Smith wrote on the opposite side of the board. "Twenty-two-years old, unemployed. Lived in a dive on the Tang Hall Estate. Found by his mother earlier today with both hands amputated. Initial path findings suggest that he also died from substantial blood loss. Kenny Bean also made a comment that the pattern of the blood spatters suggest he was standing up when his hands were removed. Similar knife in his chest after he died, and exactly the same message on his phone."

Smith stabbed the marker on the board where he had written the text message.

"This is where we need to concentrate all our efforts. These two men did not know each other - they were killed because they had both sinned."

"The amputations are important," Bridge said. "They have to be."

"I agree," Baldwin joined in. "Peter Ashe was having an affair with a schoolgirl and he had his thing chopped off. What did John Ware do to justify chopping off his hands?"

"In some Middle-East countries, they chop off the hands of thieves," Yang Chu suggested. "Maybe he was a thief."

"That's all very well and good," Smith said. "But why would someone take it upon themselves to decide to absolve these men of their sins? Who would believe they were more qualified than God to do this?"

Nobody had an answer for that.

Smith returned to the table. "This is the plan of action. I'm going to see if I can speed Kenny Bean up with that tox report – Bridge, I want you to breathe down Webber's neck to get the number of the person who sent those messages, and Baldwin, I want you to do some research about these Kila knives. Find out about suppliers. The killer must have found those knives from somewhere. Let's get moving."

CHAPTER NINETEEN

"That was more like it," Chalmers said.

He and Smith stood smoking in the car park.

"I told you," Smith said. "I've had a lot on my mind. I've still got a lot on my mind."

"I thought Whitton was out of the woods."

"It's not just that. I've done something really stupid and I don't know what to do about it."

"How long have we known each other?" Chalmers asked.

"Quite a while."

"And in that time, I've lost count of how many stupid things you've done. And you always get over it and look back and realise it wasn't the life or death stupid you thought it was at the time."

"I slept with Baldwin," Smith's mouth said before his brain could stop it.

"You stupid bastard," Chalmers said. "You stupid, stupid bastard."

"I have to tell Whitton."

"Now that *would* be stupid. What the hell were you thinking?"

"I don't know how it happened," Smith said and realised how pathetic he sounded. "We had a few drinks and..."

"Stop right there," Chalmers stubbed out his cigarette and lit another. "Now listen to me. When a story like this starts with, *we had a few drinks*, it's another kettle of fish. It's not an excuse, don't get me wrong but there is no way you are going to tell Whitton about this."

"I don't think I can live with myself if I don't."

"Don't be such a drama queen. Shit happens. Do you think you're the first bloke to stray? Don't kid yourself. It happens all the time. Problems at home, a sympathetic ear and one thing can lead to another. Add alcohol into the mix and there you have it. Baldwin? Bloody hell."

"I really think I should tell Whitton," Smith insisted.

"What for? To ease your guilty conscience? Stop being such a selfish bastard for once. What do you think will happen then? Do you think she'll forgive you and you'll live happily ever after? Don't kid yourself – things will never be the same again. You might think life will get back to normal but it'll always be there in the background, lurking. Ready to show its ugly head when you least expect it."

"I think Whitton deserves better than that," Smith wasn't quite finished yet.

"Better than what? Better than you? You're human – human's fuck up all the time, so accept it and move on. What about Baldwin? What does she think?"

"She's accepted it and moved on," Smith admitted.

"There's your answer then. Now, I don't want to hear another word about it."

"Thanks, boss."

"You stupid, stupid bastard," Chalmers said once more and walked back inside shaking his head.

As Smith drove to the hospital he made up his mind about two things. The talk with Chalmers had made him realise there are things in life that are much bigger than him. And sometimes life throws things at you that you are powerless to prevent. But it's how you deal with what's thrown at you that makes you into what you are.

Whitton was sitting up in bed when Smith came in. She had a bit more colour in her face than she had earlier. Her right arm was in a sling. Laura was sitting next to her, drawing something in a colouring book.

"There's my two favourite ladies," Smith sat in the chair next to the bed.

"How are you feeling?" he asked Whitton.

"I'll feel better when they let me out of here," she replied. "There's nothing wrong with me."

"Welcome to my world. Now you know how I felt."

"I do," Whitton said. "Back then I thought you were just being a baby, but now I can see it. Hospitals are not places to get better in. They don't leave you alone for a minute. The moment I fall asleep, I get woken up for them to ask me how I am. I'm going mad in here."

"You've only been here five minutes."

"It feels like much longer. Anyway, enough of my woes. Tell me about yours."

Smith felt his heart quicken slightly. "No woes. I need to tell you something though. Something important that is probably going to change both of our lives."

"Sounds serious."

"I'm going to accept the DI post."

Whitton didn't say anything. Laura carried on scribbling in her book.

"Don't do that," Whitton said eventually. "I'm sure the heart rate monitor just jumped twenty beats. I thought you were going to tell me you were having an affair or something. That's brilliant news."

"Nothing's set in stone yet," Smith said. "But Chalmers seems to think it's a done deal. You could soon be married to Detective Inspector Jason Smith."

Whitton laughed. "That's going to take a bit of getting used to."

"And the natural progression will mean my vacant position will be offered to you, DS Whitton."

"I like the sound of that. Any developments in the investigation?"

"There's been another one. Another man with the same message on his phone. I'll spare you the gory details seeing as though there's a three-year-old Picasso within earshot, but it wasn't pleasant. His mother found him this morning. She's here actually and I'm going to speak to her if I can."

"That's awful," Whitton stroked Laura's head. "Are we any closer to finding out what it's all about?"

"We're working on it. The DCI put a firecracker up my arse in the briefing and things are looking much more positive."

"Chalmers was always good at that. The other driver came to see me earlier."

"The arsehole?"

"He's not an arsehole. He seemed quite nice actually. He feels terrible about what happened, and he came to see how I was."

"Came to make sure you're not going to sue him more like it. Arsehole."

"He offered to pay for the damage to the car."

"Isn't that what insurance is for?"

"It's supposed to be," Whitton said. "But there's still the excess and the premiums always go up after a claim. They're sharks, insurance companies. Anyway, the guy I smashed into says he knows a really good panel-beater. They can get it fixed in no time. It saves the hassle of submitting a claim and then waiting for them to assess what happened."

"He's still an arsehole," Smith insisted.

"He made a mistake. It happens. You of all people should know about that."

"You're not wrong there," Smith mused. "Do you know when you're going to be allowed to come home?"

"They're being over-cautious," she told him. "Apparently they always are with head injuries and whiplash. Laura can go home later. My parents have offered to fetch her. They know how busy you are at the moment."

"Your parents are the best. I'd better go and speak to that bloke's mother. I'm actually supposed to be working, but I could hardly come to the hospital without popping in to say hello."

He kissed Laura on the top of the head and breathed in deeply.

Whitton shook her head. "I hope you're not still going to be doing that when she's twenty-one-years old."

"Why not?" Smith leaned over and kissed Whitton lightly on the lips. "I love the smell of her hair. I'll come back this evening to visit."

"See you later. And congratulations on the DI post. We're so proud of you."

CHAPTER TWENTY

Janet Ware sat opposite Smith in the canteen at the hospital. Smith had bought them coffee from the machine. Janet's eyes were still slightly glazed from the sedative she'd been given earlier.

"Mrs Ware," Smith began. "Thank you for speaking to me. I'm sorry about John, but I need to ask you a few questions if that's alright."

Janet nodded. "Call me Janet. Have you got them yet?"

"Mrs Ware? Sorry, Janet?"

"The scum who killed my boy. John was a good kid you know."

Smith had lost count of how many times he'd heard that from a grieving mother, or distraught father after their saintly offspring had been killed or arrested.

I've become cynical in my old age, he thought.

"He was a good kid," Janet said again. "Did well at school. Even went to sixth form. We couldn't afford it, but we made a plan. Have you got kids?"

"A little girl. She's three."

"Your time will come then."

Smith wondered exactly what she meant by that.

"Do you know if John had any enemies, Janet? Can you think of anybody who would want to hurt him?"

"I never understood why he had to move to the Tang Hall. There are places on the Hull Road much nicer. And safer. Those Tang Hall lot are evil, some of them."

"We have reason to believe where John lived had nothing to do with what happened to him," Smith told her.

Janet sipped her coffee and glanced around the canteen. A family sat at a table by the door. Two young, smiling girls were fussing over a man in a wheelchair. The girls' mother sat smiling at them. A happy family.

"John was a good kid," Janet said for the third time. "He could've gone to University you know. His A-Level mock results said he could. We could never afford it though, but we would have made a plan."

Smith was beginning to think he was wasting his time. He'd never met someone who repeated themselves so often.

"What about your husband?" he asked. "Where is he?"

Janet started to laugh. "You'll probably know more than me. He's done more time than Father Time himself. Went inside for the first time just after John was born – must have taken a liking to it, and he's been in and out ever since. I kept John away from him. John's nothing like his dad. Just got in with the wrong crowd, that's all."

Usual story then, Smith thought.

"What time did you find your son this morning?" he asked.

"Around ten. I sent him a message to let him know I was coming. I made him a homemade stew. He doesn't eat properly in that place."

Smith realised he had no more questions to ask. Janet Ware hadn't given him anything more than he already knew. The scenario unfolding before him was so familiar. Good kid get's in with the wrong crowd. Father in and out of prison – the mother tries her best to bring up her child, but history has a habit of repeating itself.

"John was a Christian, you know," Janet said out of the blue. "He really did believe. Me and his bastard father weren't churchgoers ourselves, but John never missed a Sunday. Don't know where he got it from, the belief. I suppose it means he's in heaven now doesn't it?"

"I suppose so," Smith replied. "Do you know which church he attended?"

"Some church on Marygate or Gillygate," she said. "I can't be sure which one. But he never missed a Sunday, even when he was sick as a parrot. He was a good kid."

* * *

Smith sat in his office with his eyes closed. Five words were going round and round inside his head.

He was a good kid.

Janet Ware had kept repeating those four words. If he was such a good kid, why did she have to find his body this morning? If he was such a good kid, he wouldn't have had his hands chopped off and he wouldn't have received a message about his sins.

There were still ten minutes to go before the scheduled afternoon briefing. Smith hoped the team had something new to report. The tox reports for Peter Ashe and John Ware were important as was the number of the phone that the messages were sent from.

There was a knock on the door and Chalmers came in.

"Afternoon, boss," Smith said.

"The Super wants to see you," Chalmers came straight to the point.

"I've scheduled a briefing in ten minutes. Smyth is going to have to wait."

"Smyth won't wait."

"What does he want to see me for?"

"Three words," Chalmers said. "Tang Hall Estate."

"You've got to be kidding me? I don't have time for Smyth's politics right now. Can't you tell him I'm busy?"

"The CC is breathing down his neck, Smyth is breathing down my neck and I'm afraid the neck-breathing stops with you. The Tang Hall is very delicate right now and a murder on their doorstep doesn't help. Just humour the public-school moron – who knows, it might help when you finally decide to accept the DI position."

"About that, boss," Smith said and stood up. "I'm going to go for it."

"About bloody time," Chalmers slapped Smith on the back. "Just don't wind the Super up too much."

"Would I do that? Can you head up the briefing until I get back?"

"My pleasure," Chalmers said. "It'll be like old times."

* * *

There was something different about Superintendent Smyth's office when Smith went inside. At first he couldn't quite put his finger on what it was, but then it came to him. There was no music. For as long as Smith could remember, Smyth always insisted on playing music inside his office. It was always corny, cringe-worthy music. Michael Bolton or Kenny G. Once, the Super had even asked Smith what he thought of the Andean Pan Pipe music that was blaring out of the speakers.

"Ah, Smith," the Superintendent said. "Good. Take a seat."

Smith sat down. "What's this about, sir? I was actually about to head up a briefing. We're in the middle of a murder investigation."

"That can't be helped. This is more important. I'm sure you're aware that the relationship between the police and certain low-income areas of town has become rather strained in recent times."

"I assume you're talking about Tang Hall?"

"Right. It can't go on."

"Sir?" Smith wasn't really sure what Smyth was talking about.

"Well," the Superintendent carried on. "A murder was committed on the Tang Hall Estate and I believe you are in charge of the investigation."

"That's correct, and I'd quite like to get on with it."

"All in good time. But what we need to do before then is reassure the public that we are taking this very seriously."

"I take every murder seriously, sir," Smith was seething. "It doesn't matter if the victim lives in a palace, a shack, on the streets or in a bloody car in the middle of the road. I take them all seriously."

"There's no need to get upset," Smyth said.

I'm more than fucking upset, Smith thought, and realised it wasn't that long ago he would have said the words out loud.

Think about the DI post. Think about Whitton and Laura.

He tried to calm his breathing. "What are you suggesting, sir?"

He knew what Smyth was going to say before he even said it.

"A press conference."

Smith was spot on.

"A press conference which you, as the detective in charge of the Tang Hall murder will head up."

"With all the respect due to you, sir," Smith said. "The body was only discovered this morning and as such we don't have much to tell the press right now."

"A mere technicality. The murder isn't the main issue here – it is absolutely essential that we are seen to be making this murder a priority."

"But we are, sir," Smith said.

"Are what?"

"Making it a priority, sir."

Smyth's mouth opened wide, and a gormless smile appeared on his face.

"Good. We're on the same page then. I'll set something up. You will liaise with the press officer and you'll be informed of the where and when in due course. That will be all."

CHAPTER TWENTY ONE

Smith's hand was throbbing when he walked inside the small conference room. After the meeting with Smyth, he'd punched every door on the way from the Superintendent's office to the conference room, and now his knuckles were red. He rubbed them with his other hand.

"What happened to your hand?" Bridge asked.

"Occupational hazard," Smith replied.

Chalmers smiled a knowing smile.

"Have I missed anything?" Smith said and sat down.

"Just recapping on a few things," Chalmers replied. "The chair is yours."

Smith's knuckles were really throbbing now. "Does anybody have anything new?"

"The tox reports show both men had some kind of sedative in their system," Bridge offered. "Similar to a Benzodiazepine. It appears they were drugged before they were killed."

"That clears that up then. The murderer drugs them to make it easier to carry out the amputations. Anything else?"

Yang Chu coughed. "There's something I thought about, Sarge. The second victim, John Ware – if he was drugged when his hands were chopped off, how exactly did it happen? If he was standing up, like you said?"

"Good point," Smith said and wondered why he hadn't thought the same thing. "Stand up."

"Sarge?"

"Just humour me."

Yang Chu did as he was asked.

"Stand over there," Smith pointed to the open space in front of the white board.

They both stood in front of the rest of the team.

"Right," Smith said. "You're roughly the same weight as John Ware. "Lie down on the floor."

Yang Chu shook his head and did as Smith told him.

"I don't want you to help me," Smith continued. "I want you to become a dead weight. I'm going to try and lift you up."

Yang Chu nodded. Smith picked up a marker pen from underneath the white board and grabbed Yang Chu under the arms. He tried to lift him to a standing position, all the time Yang Chu lay limp in his arms. Smith managed to get him up with some difficulty, but now he was faced with a problem. How would it be possible to chop off his hands without letting him fall to the floor? It was impossible. Smith tried holding Yang Chu with one arm while he attempted to slice at his hand with the marker pen but Yang Chu slid out of his grasp.

"You can sit down now," Smith told him.

"There were two of them," Smith said when he too sat back down. "There had to be two people there if John Ware's hands were chopped off while he was standing up. There's no other explanation."

"Great," Bridge said. "That's just doubled our workload."

"Or halved it," Smith thought out loud.

"What?"

"Theoretically, two people are easier to catch than one. If there are two of them working together, the mistakes they make will be doubled."

"If they make any mistakes," Yang Chu pointed out. "So far we haven't found anything at the scenes of any use."

"What did you find out about the knives?" Smith addressed the question to Baldwin.

"More than I expected," she said. "There are plenty of ads for these knives online. Most of them probably fake."

"How do we know if the ones left at the scene are fakes?" Bridge asked.

"You haven't checked?" Chalmers joined in.

Smith had actually forgotten the DCI was still there.

"We'll get onto it. So, how does one go about getting hold of a load of these knives?"

"Online sales, eBay, Junkmail There's more out there than I thought."

"Sarge," Yang Chu said. "John Ware had form. I checked his record. Nothing serious, but he was done for a couple of burglaries a year or so ago. Suspended sentence."

"Maybe he's still at it," Smith said. "Maybe he got a taste for it again and stole from the wrong person."

"And that person decided to rid him of his hands?" Bridge suggested.

"Could be. I spoke to his mother at the hospital. Same old story – the mother thinks the sun shines out of her kid's arse, and he can do no wrong. She didn't mention anything about the suspended sentence. She kept saying he was a good kid. Never missed a Sunday at church."

"He was a church-goer?" Bridge said.

"That's right. He probably thought that if he praised the Lord once a week his sins would be..."

"Sarge?" Yang Chu said.

"...Forgiven," Smith finished the sentence. "Do we know if Peter Ashe went to church?"

"We didn't ask," Baldwin said.

"And why would we? But we need to ask now. If Peter Ashe was a church-goer I think we've found the first connection in all of this."

"The church?" Bridge said with wide eyes.

"Why not? These murders are all about being forgiven for sins committed."

"And demons," Yang Chu reminded him.

"Christianity," Smith said. "The Devil – they're all part of the same thing really. I know it's getting late, but we need to speak to Peter Ashe's wife again."

CHAPTER TWENTY TWO

Heidi Ashe's sister, Penelope answered the door with a scowl on her face and for a moment Smith wondered if it had actually been tattooed there. It certainly complemented the steel stapled all over her face.

"What do you lot want?" the scowl deepened. "Haven't you interrogated my sister enough?"

Yang Chu looked at Smith.

"We need to ask her some more questions," Smith told her. "It shouldn't take long."

"Who is it?" a voice was heard from inside.

"Police," Penelope told her. "They were just about to leave."

"Mrs, sorry, Miss Slyper. This is extremely important. And as I said it won't take long. It's been a long day and I'd quite like to go and visit my wife at the hospital this evening. Ten minutes."

It was a cheap shot but it seemed to do the trick. Penelope opened the door wider and stepped aside.

Heidi Ashe was putting something away in a sideboard when they came in. She slammed the door shut and a framed photograph on the shelf above it jumped up and fell to the carpet with a dull thud. Smith picked it up and put it back where it was. It was a photo of a much-younger Penelope Slyper and a young man. They were standing on the edge of a sheer cliff. Behind them what appeared to be some kind of monastery was backed by a cloudless blue sky. The photo had been taken before Penelope decided she needed to set off metal detectors by inserting steel in her face. Smith recognised the man, but he couldn't remember where he had seen him before. He took a closer look. The man was tanned and a sorry excuse for a goatee beard stuck out of his chin. Smith was certain he'd seen the man somewhere before.

"Where's this?" he asked.

"I thought you were here to talk to my sister," Penelope replied.

Smith looked her in the eyes. She stared back defiantly for a few seconds then broke eye contact.

"Of course," Smith said. "Mrs Ashe, I just need to ask you if Peter was religious in any way."

"Religious?" Penelope answered for her sister. "What the hell has that got to do with anything? Are you thinking about planning his funeral? Giving him a good Christian burial?"

"Could you please leave us for a few minutes," Yang Chu said in a gentle voice. "It would be better if we talk to your sister alone. Could you do that please?"

Penelope looked at her sister and Heidi nodded.

"I'll be in the kitchen if you need me," Penelope said and left the room.

"Was Peter a religious man?" Smith asked.

"He wasn't when I met him," Heidi replied. "But he started going to church a few years ago."

"Do you know why?" Yang Chu said. "Do you know what made him suddenly decide to go to church?"

"I have no idea. I'm sorry but I don't believe in God. Never have done."

"That's your choice," Smith assured her. "So, Peter started attending church. Do you know which church it was?"

"He's always loved St Olave's on Marygate. It's old and he liked the atmosphere in there. He always used to say he felt safe surrounded by the spirits of the centuries of congregations. If that makes any sense. He used to go every Sunday but that stopped a while ago. What has this got to do with what happened to him?"

"It could be nothing," Smith said. "But we have to cover every aspect of his life. We won't take up anymore of your time."

They got ready to leave. Smith turned to Heidi Ashe.

"That photograph – the one that fell off the sideboard, where was that taken?"

Heidi stood up and took a closer look at it. "This was during Penny's gap year. She and a few of her friends hitchhiked around India, the Himalayas and China. I think this was in Tibet at some monastery. You'll have to ask her exactly where it is."

"Thank you, Mrs Ashe. We'll be in touch if we find anything new."

Smith opened the door and they went outside just as the sun was falling in the west.

"What's wrong with your wife?" Penelope Slyper was standing behind them.

"She was in a car crash," Smith told her. "She was lucky – she's going to be alright."

"You make your own luck in this world," Penelope said, and Smith walked away without saying anything further.

"That sister is definitely not right in the head," Yang Chu commented as Smith pulled away from the kerb. "I bet she's a lesbian."

"You're terrible."

"What now?"

"It's late. I'll drop you off at home and then I'm heading straight for the hospital. I promised Whitton I'd pop in and see her."

"Why do you still call her that?" Yang Chu asked. "Why do you still call her Whitton? How long have you been married?"

"It's just a habit, I suppose. I've been calling her Whitton for so long it's sort of stuck in my subconscious. I do call her Erica at times."

"I don't want to know. You can drop me off just up ahead by the shop. I need to pick up a few things before I go home. My house is just around the corner."

Smith stopped the car and Yang Chu got out.

"See you bright and early tomorrow," Smith said.

"Give my regards to Whitton," Yang Chu said in reply.

* * *

Whitton was asleep when Smith came into the hospital ward. She'd been moved from a private room to a ward and Smith took this as a sure sign she was on the mend. A young couple were talking to an old lady in the bed next to Whitton's. They were talking so quietly that Smith didn't think the old lady could even hear them. He sat next to the bed and placed his hand on Whitton's forehead. It was very warm. She stirred, changed position in the bed but she didn't wake up. Smith sat there for a while, all the time he was aware of the low murmuring coming from the people visiting the old lady in the next bed. Whitton seemed so peaceful lying there. Smith was sure she had a smile on her face.

I slept with Baldwin, Smith thought. *I slept with one of your closest friends and colleagues while you were in a car crash with our child. I'm sorry. I am so so sorry.*

He closed his eyes bowed his head and took his face in his hands.

"I'm so sorry," he realised he'd spoken out loud.

"Sorry about what?" Whitton was awake.

"I thought you were asleep."

"What are you sorry for?"

Smith had to think quickly. He wasn't quite sure how much he'd said – he couldn't even remember if he'd spoken the words about Baldwin out loud or not.

"I'm sorry I didn't take my phone with me to the Hog's head," he lied. "If I had I would have known sooner about the accident."

"You dope," Whitton sat up in bed and leaned over to kiss him on the lips.

"I assumed you were with your mum and dad," Smith added. "I was quite an arsehole to you in the briefing. Chalmers gave me a real lecture about it."

"I won't disagree with that."

"Thanks. Do you know when they're going to release you?"

Whitton started to laugh. "It's called discharge, not release. This isn't a prison you know."

"It feels like it sometimes."

"Not for another day or two. I'll just have to be patient. Besides it's not too bad in here. The old lady in the next bed is lovely. She's stone-cold deaf, so she can't hear a word I say but she loves to talk. She's had quite a life."

Smith realised that the young couple visiting her were probably not even talking to her.

"Is Laura staying with your parents tonight?" he asked.

"If that's alright. They came in earlier and Laura is acting like the crash never happened."

"She probably thought it was great fun," Smith said. "So it's just me and the dogs tonight?"

"Looks like it. Why don't you grab a bite to eat at the Hog's Head?"

"Not a chance. I'm staying put tonight. With my phone within reach."

A cheery-looking sister walked in. She smiled at Whitton as she walked past and tapped her watch.

"That's a subtle hint to tell you to bugger off," Whitton told Smith. "Visiting time is over. Get some rest – you look worse than I do."

"Thanks a lot. This investigation is draining. It's still in the early stages and I can already feel it's starting to take its toll. I'll come and see you tomorrow."

"Get something inside your stomach and get some sleep," Whitton said. "Doctor's orders. You don't want to end up in here again do you?"

Smith gave her a mock salute, kissed her on the cheek and left.

CHAPTER TWENTY THREE

Smith didn't feel like going home to an empty house. He felt like a drive, so he turned left onto Queen Street and followed Station Road across the River Ouse. The traffic was more congested here and Smith had to slow almost to a dead halt. He looked past the bridge and saw that the tourist boats were already out in full force. It was a Monday evening in early April and yet tourists were braving the weather to enjoy a sunset cruise along the river. Smith watched as a long white vessel approached the bridge and glided by underneath.

A loud hooting behind him made Smith jump, and he realised the traffic ahead of him had moved off and he was holding up the cars behind him. He sped off and joined the A19 for a short while until a sign on the side of the road made him take the next turnoff on the left. He carried on along Marygate until the Museum Gardens appeared on the left. St Olave's church was a short distance up the road. Smith slowed down and stopped next to the entrance. He was surprised to see that the gate was open and there was a light shining somewhere inside the church. He got out of the car and walked up the steps to the main entrance.

The interior of the church was dimly lit. Smith made his way down the aisle past the impressive columns that were topped with rather modern-looking archways. The altar was lit up more than the pews but a different kind of light was shining through a window in a room to the side of it. Smith made his way towards it. The door to the room was closed. Smith was about to knock when a sound from inside the room made him stop in his tracks. It was a sound that seemed out of place in a church whose origins dated back almost a millennium.

It was the unmistakable sound of a mobile phone ringtone. The ringtone stopped and Smith could hear a man's voice. The voice was very deep and

Smith couldn't make out the words. The phone conversation was very brief, and when it was over Smith knocked on the wooden door.

It was opened a short time later by a middle-aged man wearing a white shirt and a pair of brown trousers. He eyed Smith with suspicion.

"Can I help you?"

"Yes," Smith said. "My name is Detective Sergeant Smith. I'm with the York Police. I was in the area and I saw the light on."

"A police detective?" the man said.

"That's right. Do you work here?"

The man laughed. "You could put it that way." He held out his hand. "Father Jacob Swift at your service. Come in. What can I do for you?"

Smith went inside the small room. It appeared to be some kind of office. A row of filing cabinets rested against one of the walls. Against another wall stood a desk with a very expensive-looking laptop on it.

"Take a seat," Father Swift gestured to one of two chairs next to the desk.

"I'm sorry to burst in unannounced," Smith began.

"This is a church, detective. We have no set opening times here. What's this all about?"

"It's about one of your congregation. Peter Ashe."

"I heard about what happened," Father Swift said. "The poor man. Do you have any leads?"

Smith was shocked. "What did you hear?"

"That he was dead and it wasn't from natural causes. What exactly happened to him?"

"I can't go into that. So, Mr Ashe used to come to St Olave's on a Sunday?"

"For a while, yes."

"Did you know him well?"

"As well as all my parishioners. What's this all about? What has it got to do with the church?"

"I'm not sure," Smith admitted. "When was the last time you saw Mr Ashe?"

"Not for quite a long time."

"So he stopped coming to church?"

"He stopped coming to church," Father Swift repeated and frowned as though he'd thought of something else.

"Father Swift," Smith urged. "Is something wrong?"

"I just remembered. Peter came to see me on Friday."

"Why did he come on Friday?"

"I'm not sure I'm at liberty to divulge that," Father Swift said and sat up further in his chair.

"Please," Smith said. "This is very important. What was he doing in the church on a Friday?"

"He came to confess."

"How do you know it was Peter?" Smith asked. "I thought there was a screen between you and the confessor."

"There is, but I have a gift for voices. It's a curse sometimes, but once I've heard a voice I very rarely forget it."

"What time was this?"

"Early afternoon sometime. I was busy with some paperwork and I remember Peter disturbing me."

"And are you usually available to hear a confession on a Friday?" Smith asked.

"No, not normally, but I happened to be working, and Peter seemed agitated so I obliged. It didn't last long then I got back to work. With Easter around the corner there's a lot to organise, hence my presence here right now."

"What did Mr Ashe want to confess?" Smith asked even though he knew he probably wouldn't get anything out of Father Swift.

"You know I can't tell you that. What is said in the confessional is bound by confidentiality. It stays between the confessor, myself and God. Now, if you have no further questions, I'd quite like to get on."

"Did Mr Ashe confess to something to do with adultery?" Smith wasn't giving up. "An underage affair? Am I getting warmer?"

"The law has no jurisdiction in my church," Father Swift spoke with his chin raised.

"I'm afraid you're wrong there, Father," Smith informed him. "The Priest-penitent privilege does not apply in English law when a serious crime is suspected. I'll leave you to your work. Thank you for your time."

Smith got up to leave and remembered something else.

"Father Swift, do you know a man by the name of John Ware?"

The Father nodded. "John never misses a Sunday service."

"Has John confessed to anything recently?"

"I think it's time you left. I really do not appreciate being interrogated in my church."

"Thank you for your time," Smith said once more.

He left the office and walked back down the aisle. A man was sitting right at the back on one of the pews. He appeared to be praying. Smith glanced over at him and walked out of the church.

CHAPTER TWENTY FOUR

It was past nine when Smith finally opened the door and went inside his house. He realised the dogs had been locked outside all day and prepared himself for an onslaught. He opened the back door and both dogs barged in and jumped up at his waist – Fred, the gruesome Pug first, and then Theakston, the rather overweight Bull Terrier.

"I'm sorry, boys," Smith told them. "It's been a long day for me too. I suppose you're hungry?"

It wasn't a question. No sooner had Smith filled up both dog bowls they were wolfed down by a pair of canines who acted like they'd never seen food before.

Smith took a beer outside to the back garden and lit a cigarette. The past twenty-four-hours felt like they had happened to somebody else and Smith was merely there as a witness on the sidelines.

If only, Smith thought back to what had happened with PC Baldwin. *What the hell was I thinking?*

He tried to push the thought aside. He remembered Chalmers' exact words. *Shit happens. Accept that and move on.*

He wasn't sure if he would be able to do that. He was cursed with a conscience that had a habit of niggling away at his insides until he relieved the pressure somehow. Smith took a long swig from the beer bottle and shivered. He knew that when that pressure was eventually released it was never pretty.

He went back inside and turned on the oven to warm up a frozen pizza. The dogs were now fat and full and sleeping off the food they'd just eaten. While Smith waited for the oven to warm up he turned on the TV. The late edition of the news was just about to start. He went back into the kitchen and slid the pizza in the oven before it had heated up enough and went back to see what was happening in the world. Fifteen people had died in a bus crash in Saskatchewan, Canada. Donald Trump was warning English football fans to think twice about travelling to Russia for the upcoming World Cup. Smith went to fetch another beer. The local news had now started. The recent murders were naturally the top story, but as Smith watched he realised the local station didn't have much information to share. Two men had been murdered in their homes – as far as the press was aware these were two unconnected killings and the general public had no cause to panic. The bulletin lasted just over a minute and then the sport came on. Smith switched the television off and therefore didn't hear about the ongoing misfortunes of York City Football Club.

With half of the pizza uneaten on the kitchen table, Smith got another beer and went outside to the back garden. It was much cooler now and the wind was picking up. Smith hadn't bothered watching the weather forecast, and he didn't know that a nasty cold front was on its way down from Scandinavia. He shivered in his T-Shirt and cupped his hands over a cigarette to light it. The wind was getting stronger and stronger. Smith managed to light the cigarette but after three or four drags he threw it over the fence into his neighbour's garden and went back inside the house.

The dogs were now snoring in harmony on the sofa. Smith shoved Theakston to one side to make some room and sat down. The Bull Terrier didn't even stir. Smith put the beer on the coffee table, sat back and closed his eyes. The snoring dogs were getting louder now and Fred the repulsive Pug was definitely snoring off key. Smith smiled and, with the grunting lullaby in his ears he slowly drifted off to sleep.

* * *

Alex Power closed the door to the room he used as an office and locked it behind him. He switched on his laptop and licked his lips at the prospect of what was coming. While the rather outdated machine was warming up, Alex walked to the window and checked to see if he'd left any gaps in the curtains. He'd already checked them once. The blackout curtains meant that it was impossible to see inside the room from the street outside. They also ensured Alex Power could not see what was happening outside. It could be daylight outside and he would be none the wiser.

He returned to the laptop and clicked on a large file. He typed in an absurdly long password and the sub-files appeared on the screen, one by one. Alex licked his lips again and opened up the most recent one. A noise outside in the street made him jump. It was a scraping sound like somebody dragging something heavy along behind them. Alex ignored it – it was probably just a couple of cats having a fight. The new file was loading. Alex made a mental note to invest in a more modern laptop when he had the chance. He was tired of MP4s taking an age to upload.

Alex heard another noise, and this time his heart started to pound in his ears. It sounded like it came from downstairs. It couldn't be. His wife was away with work and his sixteen-year-old daughter was staying at a friend's house. Alex had the place to himself all night. He listened again, but all he could hear was the low whining of the laptop.
The MP4 had almost finished uploading.

Alex had had the brainwave a few months earlier. He'd developed a keen interest in surveillance techniques – he always fancied himself as an amateur sleuth, but this brainwave was genius. He'd researched a number of options but in the end he opted for a top-of-the-range undetectable camera. *Undetectable.*
That was what the company who sold them promised. And so far they'd lived up to that promise. The cameras were no larger than the head of a drawing pin and they came in various colours. They weren't cheap, but Alex had decided you get what you pay for and bought two on the spot. One black and one white.

He turned his attention to the image on the screen of his laptop. It was a still picture of some kind of locker room. Benches ran along the middle of the room and lockers, most of them open, filled the back of the room. Alex clicked on the triangle on the screen and settled down to watch. The still image now became a moving picture. There was no sound – Alex had decided sound wasn't necessary. On the screen people came into the frame. Or to be more precise - girls. Teenage girls, most of them naked. The position of the camera was perfect. Through trial and error and many disappointing viewing sessions, Alex had finally figured out the optimum position for both cameras. More young girls appeared, most of them glistening and freshly showered. Alex shivered with pleasure. He would watch this one back in slow motion later.

There was another sound downstairs. This time Alex knew he wasn't imagining things. It was an incessant banging noise. Somebody was hammering on the door. Alex flipped the laptop closed and got up. He unlocked the door and made sure to lock it again on the other side. The banging on the door was getting louder.

Who on earth is bothering me at this time? He thought.

It was almost ten.

He reached the front door, unlocked it and opened it, ready to give the late-night caller a piece of his mind. A man and a woman stood there. The man was very short – the woman stood a good head taller than him.

"What do you want?" Alex asked.

He was eager to get back to his laptop.

"We're here to save you." It was the woman who spoke.

Fucking Jehovah's Witnesses, Alex thought. *At this time of night.*

"I'm not interested," he said and tried to close the door.

It wouldn't close. The man had stuck his foot in the way. For a short man he had unusually large feet.

"What the hell are you doing?" Alex demanded.

"Hell is the optimum word," the woman said calmly. "Now could you please let us in so we can help you?"

"Fuck off," Alex said and tried to kick the man's feet away.

He felt a burning sensation in his thigh. He looked down and saw there was a syringe sticking out at a right angle to his leg.

"What the hell," he said once more.

His whole leg now felt numb and he was having difficulty standing on it. He felt himself being pushed inside his house and he heard the door slam. He was helped inside the living room and shoved onto the sofa. The numbness in his leg had now spread to his stomach and he was sure he could feel its coolness moving up to his chest. He was aware of noises inside the room – voices, but he couldn't quite decipher the words.

Alex felt his head being jerked back and then he felt the most intense pain he had ever experienced. Something sharp had been stuck inside his eye. The sedative he'd been given hadn't had enough time to completely numb all his senses and he could feel the sensation of the scalpel rummaging around in his eye socket. The pain was white-hot now. He tried to raise his hands but they wouldn't obey.

"God has forgiven you your sins," the man spoke with a deep voice.

Alex heard these words. Then he screamed as his other eyeball was gouged out.

"But He could not rid you of your demons, so I have taken them for you."

Without his eyes, Alex couldn't see what was going to happen next. He could feel the blood seeping out of the gaping holes where his eyes once were, but he couldn't see what the man was doing. The numbness had almost taken over his whole body now. He heard the sound of a mobile phone ringtone and a few moments later he heard the familiar sound of his own message notification tone.

Through the numbness Alex sensed movement close by, then he was aware of a dull ache in his chest. He could feel his heartbeat in his ears as it slowed down then finally stopped.

CHAPTER TWENTY FIVE

Smith opened his eyes and realised he was covered in dogs. Even though he knew there were only two of them, it felt like three times that. Legs stuck out from all angles, and a tail lay across Smith's face. He shrugged the limbs away and stood up. He was fully dressed and he felt cold. One of the windows looking out onto the back garden had been left open and the curtains were billowing in the wind like racing spinnakers.

"That's why you two decided to take liberties in the night," Smith spoke to the two stretching forms on the sofa. "You can't handle a bit of cold."

Both dogs jumped off and ambled into the kitchen, clearly in search of breakfast.

Smith looked at the clock on the mantelpiece. It was not yet seven but he felt refreshed. Dogs or no dogs, he'd slept for longer than he had for quite some time. He went outside for the first cigarette of the day and came straight back inside. The cold wind was biting and he was dressed only in a T-Shirt and jeans. He grabbed a coat, put it on and opened the back door again. With great difficulty he managed to light a cigarette and he went around the side of the house where it was more sheltered. This was more like the English spring he remembered. The recent warm weather had just been a passing illusion.

As he sipped his coffee inside the warmth of the kitchen Smith thought about his conversation with Father Swift. There was something that was niggling away at him about Father Swift. It wasn't so much what he'd said, but a combination of his reaction to Smith's questions and what he hadn't actually said. Smith made a mental note to make it a priority to confirm what he'd told the Father at St Olave's. He wasn't a hundred percent certain about the law where the Priest-penitent privilege was concerned. He didn't know many lawyers, and he'd bumped heads with a fair few over the years so he decided the best thing to do would be to trust in Google. Something else was bothering him. Peter Ashe made a confession at St Olave's Church early afternoon on Friday. A few hours later he was dead. That had to be more than coincidence.

Smith was debating whether to make another cup of coffee when his doorbell rang. He switched on the kettle anyway and went to see who it was. Yang Chu was standing on the doorstep holding his face away from the wind.

"What's wrong?" Smith asked him.

"Apart from a Baltic gale-force wind, nothing," Yang Chu replied. "Can I at least come inside?"

"Sorry," Smith let him past. "Has something happened?"

"I just woke up too early and didn't want to go in to work yet. Is that the click of the kettle boiled?"

"You want a cup?"

"I thought you'd never ask."

Smith made them both coffee and they sat down at the kitchen table. Yang Chu sat quietly and stared around the room.

"What is it you really came here for?" Smith asked him.

"I told you, I…"

"Don't bullshit me. Out with it."

"It's just the other night," Yang Chu spoke in the direction of the back door. "When Whitton had her accident. Where were you really?"

"What are you talking about?"

"You said you were at the Hog's Head. I forgot to mention that I thought about that and I checked. The owner said you left ages before. You weren't at home and you weren't at your local pub."

"I'd mind my own business if I were you," Smith said. "Where I was that night has nothing to do with you."

"Fair enough. I was just curious that's all."

"Downright bloody nosey more like it," Smith said. "Finish your coffee – we've got a lot to go through this morning. I have some new theories I want to bring up."

"I don't like the sound of that."

Superintendent Jeremy Smyth pounced on Smith as soon as he walked through the doors of the station. Smith was gobsmacked – Smyth very rarely arrived before ten and even then he immediately made a beeline for his office where he often stayed cooped up for a further few hours.

"Smith," Smyth said. "Good, you're here bright and early. I have some good news about the press conference."

The words, good news and press conference cannot possibly be used in the same sentence, Smith thought.

"I've had second thoughts about that, sir," Smith said. "I really don't think it's such a good idea this early in the investigation."

"Nonsense," Smyth said with a dramatic shake of the head. "And do I need to remind you how essential press conference savvy is in the modern Police Force – especially as one rises up the ranks if you get my drift."

With this he smiled at Smith and tapped his nose. Yang Chu looked on, bewildered.

"Where and when?" Smith sighed.

He turned to Yang Chu and rolled his eyes.

"Nothing like an early bird to catch the early worm," Smyth said. "I've scheduled it for ten this morning. Two hours from now."

That explains Smyth's mysterious early start, Smith thought.

"We are in the middle of a murder investigation," Smith reminded him.

"Yes. The press liaison officer is expecting you. We're expecting quite a crowd this morning. Break a leg."

With that he shuffled off in the direction of his office.

"That man is a total idiot," Smith said to Yang Chu. "I didn't think he could get any worse, but he seems to leak more brain cells with each passing year."

Yang Chu laughed. "Rather you than me, Sarge. What was all that stuff about rising up the ranks? That cloak and dagger bollocks?"

"You may be looking at the new DI. It's not definite, but Brownhill's position has been pretty much offered to me."

"Congratulations."

"Don't congratulate me yet," Smith said. "Like I said it's not set in stone, and I still need to work on my press conference savvy first. Wish me luck."

CHAPTER TWENTY SIX

Neil Walker was typing so quickly on his laptop that Smith couldn't believe it was physically possible. The press liaison officer didn't look up when Smith came in – he continued to type at lightning speed.

"Take a seat," he said and carried on with what he was working on.

Smith sat opposite him at the desk. "Did you have to do a special course to be able to type like that? I still haven't graduated from two finger jabbing."

Walker stopped what he was doing. "I taught myself. After a while you can imagine the words in your head and they somehow just appear on the screen. Anyway, it's a good job I can type like this – Old Smyth didn't give me much warning. A press release two hours before the conference isn't exactly common practice. I suppose that's why they pay me the big bucks."

"Me too," Smith said. "Smyth told me to speak to you."

Walker stretched his arms and wriggled his fingers. "You know more than me about the current investigation, but what Smyth has in mind is not so much the murder itself but the emphasis on the prioritisation of the Tang Hall Estate."

"I've already told the bungling idiot that we take all murders seriously, regardless of the postal code."

"I don't doubt you did," Walker said. "But you have to see it from his point of view."

"Put myself in the head of an amoeba, you mean?"

Walker laughed. "Something like that. You and I are mere pawns in all of this. Even Smyth is just a chess piece that those higher up on the food chain use to achieve their objectives. The Tang Hall Estate is a political matter. A murder on the Tang Hall can be used by these politicians. It can turn in their favour or it can go the other way, depending on how they spin it. Do you understand what I'm saying?"

"Loud and clear. So, what is it Smyth expects me to tell these journos?"

"I'll give you a print-out of the press release. Have a look at it before you go in there, but what you need to hammer home is – low-income estate or not, you are working night and day to bring this matter to its swift conclusion."

"That's what we *are* doing," Smith was getting tired of repeating himself. "But so far we don't have much to tell the press. It's still early days."

"Do you have any leads?"

"A few that we're looking into, but nothing we can make public just yet."

"Then you are following up on a number of enquiries. Any suspects as yet?"

"One comes to mind," Smith told him. "But until we dig a bit further, we can't mention any names."

Smith knew if Father Jacob Swift's name came up the press would have a field day.

"OK," Walker said. "We haven't got much time left. Give them the old spiel. *We are following up on a number of enquiries* and *we're still waiting for the final results to come in*. That sort of crap but emphasise the effort you and you team are putting in on the Tang Hall Estate. The sole objective of this press conference is to highlight the fact that the Police absolutely do not discriminate against anyone. Rich or poor, we treat all crimes equally."

"It's a load of bullshit really isn't it?"

"Isn't it just?" Walker said. "Read over the release and just answer the questions honestly. You'll do just fine."

* * *

Smith leaned closer to the microphone. The crowd of people in front of him had switched on their recording devices and were all eager to hear what he had to say. Smith had to admit he was impressed with how Superintendent Smyth had managed to round up so many representatives of the press in such a short time. Smyth sat next to Smith with an inane grin on his face. The Superintendent lived for press conferences.

"Good morning," Smith began. "Thank you all for coming at such short notice. I'm sure you are all aware that two murders have been committed in the past few days. Two men were killed in their homes. We're not certain the murders are connected at this stage, but we are following up on a number of leads and we are making steady progress."

A man in the front row stuck up his hand. "Can you tell us more about the murders? How were these men killed?"

"I'm not able to divulge the details at the moment," Smith said. "Until we have the final autopsy reports I wouldn't like to speculate."

"Peter Ashe and John Ware," a woman two rows back shouted. "That's already common knowledge."

The power of social media, Smith thought.

"That's right," Smith admitted. "Two men from different parts of town and two men who didn't know each other as far as we're aware."

"John Ware lived on the Tang Hall Estate didn't he?" the woman said.

Smith felt a slight tap under the table. Smyth had kicked him and it was rather unnerving.

"That is correct," he said. "And Peter Ashe lived on the other side of town."

"The well-fed side?" a young man with long hair said.

"Was that a question?" Smith asked.

"It was more a statement of fact," the man said. "Sven Mink, York Uni blog."

I never would have guessed, Smith thought.

"One victim on the right side of town and one on the other – I assume you're treating both murders equally?"

"Your assumption would be correct."

Smith didn't like the direction this was heading in.

"Come on, detective," Mink continued. "A bloke dies on the Tang Hall. It's one less scumbag for you to deal with, admit it."

"I'll say this once," Smith could feel his face reddening. "And once only. When I investigate a murder, I look at a number of elements. Evidence, motive, opportunity etc. Where the victim happened to live is irrelevant."

"Yeh right," the University blogger said with a sneer.

"Right," Smith looked directly at him. "My job is to catch criminals. People who break the law. In a murder investigation, I treat all victims equally. Whether they are royalty, doctors, shop assistants, even journalists."

There were a few sniggers in the crowd.

Superintendent Smyth cleared his throat loudly and Smith took this as an indication he wanted to say something.

"If I may," Smyth said. "The two murders are not the significant factor here."

Smith grimaced. He wanted a trapdoor to open underneath him and swallow him up.

"Are you saying that the fact that two men were killed is not significant?" It was Sven Mink.

"Um, no," Smyth mumbled. "No, of course not. What's important here is the fact that York Police are taking them both seriously. It doesn't matter that one of the victims lived on an undesirable estate."

"I live on the Tang Hall Estate," a man holding up an iPhone commented. "Some of us don't have much choice in the matter."

"Of course," Smyth said. "I didn't mean it like that. What I meant to say is what DS Smith has emphasised already."

"Which is?"

Smyth opened his mouth to say something and a gormless grin appeared on his face.

"Superintendent?" the man with the iPhone urged.

"I think we've covered everything for today," Smith stepped in before Smyth could do any more damage. "Thank you all for coming."

He stood up and left the room leaving a bunch of unsatisfied journalists in his wake.

CHAPTER TWENTY SEVEN

Smith was looking through the pathology report on John Ware in his office when Smyth came in.

"My office now," the Superintendent barked.

"I'm busy," Smith said and carried on looking at the screen.

"You made me look like a complete fool back there," Smyth's voice changed pitch. "You left me in front of those vultures looking like an idiot."

"I don't have time for this, *sir*," Smith turned around and told him. "And I do not appreciate having my time wasted in the middle of a double murder investigation."

Smith tried to calm his breathing but the mere presence of Smyth in his office was making it impossible.

He turned his attention back to the screen.

"The whole purpose of the press conference was to reassure the public that the police are on the side of the low-income estates, and that debacle back there had the opposite effect."

Smyth was now talking to Smith's back.

Smith breathed in deeply and kept quiet.

"Don't you have something to say?" Smyth said.

Smith shook his head.

What happened next would stay in Smith's memory for the rest of his life. Superintendent Smyth approached Smith, grabbed him by the shoulders and forcefully turned him so they were facing each other.

"Look at me when I'm talking to you," Smyth said in a voice Smith had never heard come out of his mouth before.

"Get your hands off me," Smith said and shrugged the hands away. "And let's get a couple of things straight. One, I did not make you look like a complete fool because you did a perfectly good job of that on your own.

Two, I did not leave you with those vultures looking like an idiot because you *are* an idiot. You didn't need any more help from me."

Smyth took a step closer. He had a wild look in his eyes that Smith found quite unsettling. Then he did something that took Smith completely by surprise.

The blow wasn't hard, but it still made Smith see flashes of light for a few seconds. Smith was more stunned than hurt. Superintendent Jeremy Smyth, the public-school buffoon had just punched him in the face just under his left eye. Smyth moved his arm back and Smith could see he was getting ready to aim another punch. Smith beat him too it. In a flash he was on his feet – he stepped back a few feet and landed a right hook under the Superintendent's jaw. Smyth's head snapped back and he swaggered backwards a couple of paces. Smith hit him again, this time on his right cheekbone.

The whole surreal episode lasted barely thirty seconds. It was clear that Smyth had no more fight left in him. He rubbed his cheek and pointed a bony finger at Smith.

"You're finished. You are well and truly fucked."

He staggered out of the room.

Smith sat for a while staring blankly at the computer screen. He wasn't actually looking at what was on the screen, he was somewhere else entirely. What had just happened with the Superintendent didn't seem real, and if the consequences of him hitting Smyth weren't so dire the whole thing would actually be quite comical. Leaving the pathology report on the screen, he left the office. He needed a smoke.

The wind was even stronger when Smith got outside. It was coming directly from the north. Smith went round the side of the station where it was more sheltered and found Chalmers there. The DCI obviously had the same idea.

Smith lit a cigarette and inhaled. The nicotine started to work and he felt his breathing get back to normal.

"Bloody awful weather," Chalmers stated the obvious. "How did the press conference go?"

"It'll probably be my last," Smith replied rather vaguely.

"That bad?"

"Smyth made a total balls-up of the whole thing. The man is a liability to the police."

"He is, isn't he? The press are used to him by now. It'll all be forgotten about in a couple of days."

"Probably," Smith took a long drag of his cigarette.

"What's up?" Chalmers asked. "I know that look."

"Smyth punched me."

Chalmers started to cough. He'd been halfway through inhaling his cigarette. He coughed a few more times and his eyes began to water.

"The Super punched me," Smith said. "It wasn't much of a punch – my three-year-old daughter probably could have hit harder but he smacked me one."

Chalmers started to laugh.

"It's not funny, boss," Smith said.

"I thought your face looked different. Your eye is a bit swollen. Smyth has just gone up in my estimation tenfold."

"I hit him back, boss." Smith told him and Chalmers stopped laughing.

"I hit him twice," Smith added. "Once under the chin and once on his cheekbone. He's not happy. He all but told me to start looking for another job."

"It'll blow over," Chalmers said. "He hit you first, remember. Did anyone see this happen?"

"That's the problem, boss. It was just me and him in my office. It'll be his word against mine. He looked really pissed off. I've never seen him like that before."

"I'll have a word with him when he's calmed down a bit. This is a turn up for the books. Superintendent Jeremy Smyth smacked one of his detective sergeants."

"Do you really think it'll blow over? That I've got nothing to worry about?"

"I promise you, he'll be more embarrassed than anything, and he won't want anybody to know about it. You mark my words."

CHAPTER TWENTY EIGHT

Chalmers' words were all but forgotten as Smith sat once more in the small conference room. The press contingency had left with little more than what they had already gleaned from social media and Smith knew that would only lead to one thing.

Speculation.

And speculation was never a good thing when they were in the middle of a murder investigation. Speculation tended to bring the weirdos out of the woodwork – the regular callers who claimed to have important information about the crimes. Ninety-nine percent of the time, their information yielded nothing apart from wasted police hours.

"Let's get started," Smith said. "We're a bit behind schedule because of the press conference, so we need to do some catching up."

"How did it go?" Bridge asked.

"Same as usual," Smith replied. "A total waste of time."

"What happened to your eye?" Yang Chu had noticed the slight swelling.

"Long story. Before we recap, there's something I stumbled upon that I think is important. Peter Ashe and John Ware didn't know each other but there is one thing they had in common. They both attended the same church – St Olave's on Marygate."

"A lot of people go to church," Bridge argued.

"Hear me out. I spoke to the Reverend there yesterday - Father Swift and he told me something interesting. Both Ashe and Ware had been there recently to confess."

"So they confessed," Bridge was obviously in an argumentative mood today. "It still doesn't mean the church is involved."

"Bridge," Smith said. "Shut up. Peter Ashe confessed to something mid-afternoon on Friday. He was killed a few hours later. Now does anybody else think that's more than just coincidence?"

"You hate coincidences," Yang Chu said.

"Exactly. Two or three hours after Ashe confessed, he was murdered."

"Do we know what he confessed to?" Baldwin asked.

"Father Swift wouldn't tell me."

"And you can't make him," Bridge said. "They've got this priest-client confidentially thing like doctors and lawyers."

"That's where you're wrong," Smith said. "I still need to confirm it, but the Priest-penitent privilege doesn't apply in English law when a serious crime is suspected."

"Are you sure?" Bridge said.

"What is your problem today?" Smith asked. "Why do you have to contradict everything I say?"

"Just because you're heading up the investigation doesn't make you right. And you seem to keep forgetting my rank."

"Like I said," Smith ignored him. "I'll have to double-check but I'm almost certain about the privilege and if that's the case Father Swift will have to tell us about the confession."

"What if he doesn't?" Bridge hadn't quite finished yet. "Are we going to arrest a Vicar for withholding information? That's going to look bloody marvellous in the papers isn't it?"

"Just shut the hell up," Smith shouted and the three detectives around the table stared at him. "You are not helping. We will speak to Father Swift again. Peter Ashe confessed to something and I'm certain that confession is extremely relevant to this investigation."

"Are you suggesting Father Swift is involved somehow?" Baldwin asked.

"I sincerely hope he isn't," Smith said. "But right now, all leads point to that church. Does anybody have anything else to add?"

"I checked places where you can buy the Kila knives," Baldwin said. "And there are so many of them that there simply aren't enough hours in the day to check them all. They could have been bought overseas for all we know."

"We'll leave that for now then," Smith agreed. "Let's look at what we do know. Peter Ashe had a thing for teenage girls – his manhood was lopped off shortly after confessing something to Father Swift. I believe his confession had something to do with adultery or an affair with an underage girl. Agreed?"

He looked around the table. Everyone including Bridge nodded.

"And," Smith continued. "John Ware was also part of Father Swift's congregation. He was a known thief and his hands were chopped off."

"But he didn't confess to anything," Yang Chu pointed out.

"No," Smith said. "We don't know whether he did or not. But we're going to find out. And if it turns out that he did make a confession shortly before he was killed then we have ourselves a clear link between these two men. Bridge, you can come with me. Maybe some time in church will quell some of the skepticism that appears to be oozing out of you today. Baldwin, I want you to look into the Priest-penitent privilege – if that privilege doesn't apply in this country, I want to bring that to Father Swift's attention. I'll haul him in here and interview him formally if I have to. Yang Chu, you get over to forensics. I don't know what's going on there at the moment, but they're slowing us down."

"What am I supposed to do there?" Yang Chu asked.

"Find out what's taking so long. Webber's guys have had Peter Ashe's and John Ware's mobile phones for days now and they haven't given us anything. Get onto it."

"What's wrong with you today?" Bridge asked Smith outside in the car park. "You're even more grumpy than usual."

"I'm not grumpy," Smith protested. "I'm just getting a bit tired of being a one-man CID team."

"What the hell is that supposed to mean?"

"Smith, head up the press conference. Smith, spoon-feed these imbeciles because they've left their brains at home today. Smith, hold DS Bridge's hand because he isn't a detective sergeant's arse. I'm getting sick of it."

"What did you say?" Bridge asked.

"I'm getting sick of it."

"I do not need anybody to hold my hand," Bridge said. "You think you're some big shot because you got lucky solving a few cases. You've turned into a real arrogant prick."

"I'd keep my mouth shut if I were you."

"What are you going to do?" Bridge's face had turned red. "Suspend me? In case you've forgotten I was promoted not so long ago, but you probably didn't notice because you had your head so far up your own arse you couldn't tell if it was day or night."

"Don't push me, Rupert."

That was all it took. Smith never used Bridge's Christian name unless it was to ridicule or provoke. And on this occasion the latter was certainly the case. Bridge grabbed him by the collar and shoved him backwards. Smith moved in and swung a punch. Bridge was much more agile than Smyth had been – he dodged out of the way and landed his own fist in almost exactly the same place the Superintendent had hit him earlier. This blow was much harder and Smith blacked out for a second. When his vision returned, he saw red. Where Bridge's face was, Smith only saw a circle of deep crimson. He clenched his fist and hit Bridge with everything he had. He hit him so hard than when the fist connected Smith was sure he had broken it. Bridge fell backwards and hit the tarmac.

Smith knew he should have left it at that. He'd done enough damage, but the part of his brain that analysed reason didn't seem to be working properly. He moved closer to Bridge and was about to lean over and give him another smack when he felt a hand on his shoulder and he was roughly pulled away.

"What the hell is wrong with you, Smith?" It was Chalmers.

He'd come outside for a smoke.

Smith rubbed his cheekbone. Chalmers held out his hand to help Bridge up but Bridge shrugged it off and stood up without it.

"What the hell is wrong with you?" Chalmers asked Smith again. "First you deck the Super, and now you're brawling with one of your closest friends and colleagues in the car park."

"You decked Smyth?" Bridge asked.

Even though he was clearly in pain, Bridge now had what appeared to be a smile on his face.

"You decked old Smyth?"

"He hit me first," Smith explained. "I gave him a couple of slaps to warn him off."

"I wish I could have seen that," Bridge said and put his hand under his chin where Smith had hit him. "That's quite a right hook you've got there."

"Sorry about that," Smith said.

"Me too."

Chalmers was shaking his head. "Now you've both got that out of your systems, Smith, go home."

"Boss?" Smith said.

"Go home. I spoke to Smyth and he's not backing down. Even though he hit you first he's still baying for your blood. I'll have another word with him when he's calmed down a bit more, but you need to get as far away from here as possible. Take a few days off. Spend some time with your wife."

"We're in the middle of a murder investigation," Smith reminded him. "We're short staffed as it is."

"And it'll do none of us any good if you get fired. The Super is talking along those lines. Take a few days off and calm down."

"Are you suspending me?"

"If that's what it takes," Chalmers said. "You stupid bastard. You realise you've probably just blown any chance of that DI post don't you?"

"You know what, boss?" Smith said. "Right now, I really couldn't give a shit."

CHAPTER TWENTY NINE

Sophie Power froze in her tracks when she spotted her dad's van parked in the driveway. She couldn't figure out why it was still there – he was supposed to be at work. Sophie had slept over at a friend's house – a large quantity of alcohol had been consumed and as a result neither Sophie nor her friend had made it to school that morning. Sophie was sixteen years old, and in her final year of school. She'd been allowed to stay over with her friend on the condition that they would study for the upcoming GCSE exams. That hadn't happened of course. Sophie had woken that morning with a stinking headache and a very delicate stomach.

The sight of her father's van in the driveway didn't help Sophie's head or her stomach. She didn't know what to do – she'd walked a long way and all she wanted now was to curl up in bed and sleep. She thought quickly. She could lie to her father and tell him they didn't have class today and they had been told to study at home. He might believe her or he might not. Her head was throbbing now and she made up her mind.

She turned the door handle and opened the door. She went inside the house and closed the door as quietly as she could. She'd only walked a few steps down the hallway when she smelled it. An unpleasant odour with a slightly metallic edge to it. Her stomach rumbled and she took a few deep breaths through her mouth. She went into the kitchen and poured a glass of water. Her stomach was really bubbling now so she took small, safe sips. The house was silent. There was no indication that her dad was home.

Sophie sipped more water and felt her mouth was suitably moist to take a couple of headache tablets. She popped them in her mouth and managed to swallow both with some more water. She put the glass in the sink and walked towards the living room. The unpleasant smell was still there. It seemed thicker, more oppressive the closer she came to the living room. The door was open and she went inside.

Alex Power was sitting on the sofa opposite the large TV. When Sophie got closer she realised straight away that even if the TV was switched on her father wouldn't be able to watch it. There were two black holes where his eyes once were. Black stripes covered his face and for one moment he reminded Sophie of a particularly repulsive circus clown she'd seen when she was little. With a face covered in black and white stripes, the clown had given her nightmares for weeks afterwards.

Alex Power had something sticking out of his chest. It was long and black and shaped like a dragon. Sophie looked at his face again. She could see something that looked like dark-red jelly in the black eye sockets. She felt a burning sensation in her stomach and fell to her knees. She lunged forwards and retched. She retched until there was nothing left inside her stomach. The vomit was all liquid apart from two perfectly intact headache tablets.

It took Sophie Power more than an hour to raise the alarm. She managed to get to her feet, drag herself to the house next door and ring the doorbell. When her neighbour opened the door, Sophie was sobbing uncontrollably. When she finally calmed down and explained what had happened the neighbour helped her inside and phoned the police.

Chalmers and Bridge arrived at the scene twenty minutes later. Grant Webber pulled up a short time later with Harry, his technician and Yang Chu in tow. The young DC had been talking to Webber when the call came through. Smith was conspicuous in his absence. Chalmers and Bridge got out the car and Webber approached them.

"Bob," he said to Chalmers. "Office being spring-cleaned is it?"

"Very funny," Chalmers said. "I do get out when I can."

"Where's Smith?" the Head of Forensics asked.

"Taking some time off," Chalmers said and didn't elaborate. "Do we know what we've got yet?"

"Your guess is as good as mine. I just got a call to say we've got a body. That's all I know. Who called it in?"

"Woman at number eight," Bridge told him. "She said she answered the door and found a young girl on her doorstep in a right state. Blabbering about her Dad being dead."

"Let's go and have a look then."

Chalmers and Bridge followed Webber and Harry inside number ten.

"It's that smell again," Webber said. "I'd know that smell anywhere."

"Blood," Chalmers added. "Bridge, you and Yang Chu check upstairs. Let us old-timers stay down here."

"Speak for yourself," Webber said and walked into the living room.

"In here," he called to Chalmers.

"Bloody hell," Chalmers looked at the man on the sofa. "What the hell happened to him?"

"His eyes are gone," Webber stated the obvious. "And... It's another one." He pointed to the ornate handle sticking out of his chest.

"No sign of a struggle," Chalmers commented. "This place is spotless."

"There won't be," Webber said. "Any sign of a struggle, I mean, because he was drugged first. We need to look for a mobile phone."

"There's one on the sideboard here," Chalmers said. "The light's flashing. I'll leave you to it."

Bridge and Yang Chu came back down the stairs.

"There's nothing we could see up there," Bridge said. "One of the rooms was locked so we couldn't check it. Did you find him?"

"In the living room," Chalmers replied. "Not a pretty sight. His eyes have been removed and there's a strange knife sticking out of his chest."

"Another one then," Yang Chu said.

"Do we know who he is?" Bridge asked.

"We'll find out," Chalmers said. "We'll need to speak to his daughter. Poor girl. What a sight to come home to."

"Was there a message on his mobile phone?" Yang Chu asked.

"Webber's checking it," Chalmers replied.

"Don't let his assistant get his hands on it."

"Why not?"

"The stupid idiot misplaced the other two phones. The ones we found at Peter Ashe's and John Ware's houses. Reckons he doesn't know where they disappeared to. That's why it's taken so long to get a trace on the number the message was sent from."

"I bet Webber loved that," Chalmers said. "Evidence going missing."

"The moron should be fired for that," Bridge joined in. "It wasn't just evidence; it was vital evidence."

"Maybe the phones will turn up," Chalmers said. "They can't have just disappeared into thin air. Let's go and see if the daughter has anything to tell us."

CHAPTER THIRTY

Smith was oblivious to what had happened to Alex Power. He was driving for the sake of driving. He didn't even realise it when he drove past the fishmonger on Green Street for the third time in the space of an hour. All he wanted to do was drive. He didn't understand what was happening to him. He'd managed to punch two of his colleagues in the space of an hour or two, and the thought was quite disturbing. Smyth had initiated the altercation, but even then Smith knew he had gone too far, and it could turn out to be a costly mistake. Bridge on the other hand was something entirely different. Bridge had merely spoken the truth and Smith had let him have it.

"What the hell is happening to me?" He asked himself in the rearview mirror.

It was as he was passing the fishmonger for the fourth time that he knew. He knew what this was all about but the only way to put an end to it could turn out to be disastrous. He was lashing out because of what had happened that night at Baldwin's flat – his conscience was ripping him apart inside, and the only way he knew how to deal with it was to let off steam in other ways. He realised that he couldn't go on much longer like this. Something was bound to snap inside him that would cause more damage than was humanly possible to undo. He could end up losing everything. There was only one thing he could do.

* * *

Whitton looked wide awake when Smith walked into the ward. Her eyes were much brighter and all the colour had returned to her face. Her green eyes sparkled when she spotted Smith.

"Hey, you. Haven't you got a job to go to?"

"I'm bunking off," Smith said. "How are you feeling?"

"Like I'm taking up a hospital bed some sick person could use. I feel like a phony. There's nothing wrong with me. I can get out of bed and walk around now and I'm actually starting to enjoy the food in here."

"That's never a good sign," Smith said. "Are you allowed to leave the ward?"

"Of course. But I don't think there's any free rooms at the moment if you're thinking what I'm thinking."

"Mrs Smith, you have a filthy mind. Let's get some fresh air."

"They're probably going to discharge me later today

They went outside to the car park and found an area that was sheltered from the wind. Whitton sat down on one of the benches there. Smith lit a cigarette and thought about what he was going to say.

"How's the investigation going?" Whitton asked. "Anything new?"

"Would you believe my number one suspect right now is a certain Father Jacob Swift of St Olave's Church?"

Whitton laughed. "Nothing surprises me about you anymore."

"I've got something I need to tell you," Smith stubbed out his cigarette and sat down next to Whitton.

"Is it about the DI job?"

"Not exactly. I did something really stupid today. Two things actually. Old Smyth really messed up in the press conference this morning."

"Nothing new there then."

"I mean it was a real balls-up. Even by Smyth's standards. Anyway, he barged in my office afterwards and made out it was my fault he ended up looking like a fool."

"You're joking?" Whitton still had a smile on her face.

"He wouldn't let it drop, so I told him I had a lot of work to do and turned my back on him."

"I bet he loved that?"

"No," Smith said. "He didn't. "He spun me round and punched me in the face.

Whitton's smile faded. "Has he totally lost the plot?"

"That's not all," Smith said. "I hit him back. Twice."

The smile returned. "Good on you. I think I would have done the same. You're not going to get into trouble for it are you? It was Smyth who threw the first punch."

"It's his word against mine. Chalmers reckons I can kiss the DI position goodbye."

"We'll fight it. Smyth was in the wrong."

Whitton wasn't exactly making it easy for Smith to say what he had to say next. He lit another cigarette.

"Me and Bridge had a fight in the car park shortly afterwards. We made friends almost straight afterwards, but a few punches were thrown."

"Two fights in one day," Whitton said. "That's got to be a record."

"I'm lashing out, Erica," Smith said. "I'm letting off steam because of what's happening inside me. I'm scared I might do something that I won't be able to come back from."

"What are you talking about?" Whitton said. "You're scaring me now."

Smith decided to just get it over with. To stand on the edge of the sheer cliff and jump.

"The night of your accident," he said.

He was looking over the edge at the ground below.

"I wasn't at home and my phone battery didn't die. I went to the Hog's Head and had something to eat. I left my phone at home."

"You don't have to feel guilty about leaving your phone at home. It happens."

"I bumped into Baldwin and we sat and had a few drinks."

The freefall had begun.

"It was actually more than a few drinks. I was very drunk. I walked her home and she invited me in for coffee. We got chatting and we kissed." The ground was getting closer and closer now.

"You kissed Baldwin?" Whitton said. "You kissed PC Baldwin. What were…"

"Erica," Smith said. "Stop. I didn't just kiss her. I wouldn't be exploding like this with people I care about because of one kiss. I spent the night. I slept with Baldwin."

Smith hit the ground and realised that the life he had before was about to change forever.

CHAPTER THIRTY ONE

"Sophie," Chalmers spoke in a gentle voice. "My name is Detective Chief Inspector Chalmers, and this is my colleague, Detective Sergeant Bridge. How are you feeling?"

Chalmers and Bridge sat in the living room of Sophie Powers' next-door-neighbour. Yang Chu had stayed next door. Chalmers had told him to have a closer look around the house. Debbie Hill, the neighbour was sitting next to Sophie on the sofa.

"Sophie?" Chalmers said.

"I can't get it out of my head," she said. "His eyes."

She started to sob. Chalmers waited until she calmed down a bit.

"I know this is hard, Sophie, but could you tell us what happened when you got home?"

"I nearly didn't go inside the house. I was supposed to be at school, but me and Katie had a few bottles of wine last night and we both felt like hell this morning."

"Katie?" Bridge said.

"Katie Holloway. My best friend. My dad said I could sleep over if I promised to study."

"What time did you get home?" Chalmers asked.

"Around half-ten. I saw my dad's van in the drive and wondered why he wasn't at work. He was supposed to be working at some school re-doing their whole plumbing. I felt terrible so I decided to go inside. I took a couple of headache tablets and went into the living room. That's when..."

She started to cry again.

"It's alright, Sophie," Bridge said. "Where's your mother?"

"She's away for work. She goes away a lot. She's a dental rep. Why would someone do that? Why would someone do that to his eyes?"

"We're going to find out," Chalmers promised. "Has your mother been contacted?"

"I got hold of her employer," Debbie told him. "They're going to tell her what happened. Sophie can stay with me until she gets back."

"We'll leave you to get some rest," Chalmers said.

He and Bridge went next door. Yang Chu was talking to Grant Webber in the hallway. Yang Chu was very red in the face. Webber's technician stormed out of the house and hurried towards his car.

"What's going on?" Chalmers asked.

"Your DC has just attacked my technician," Webber told him.

"You did what?" Chalmers said to Yang Chu.

"I didn't attack him. I just asked him how it was possible to misplace two vital pieces of evidence."

"You called him an imbecile," Webber elaborated.

"He is," Yang Chu said. "How can you have somebody on your team who loses important evidence? Those phones could have led us straight to the killer."

"Mistakes happen," Webber said.

"That wasn't a mistake," Yang Chu said. "That was a king-sized balls-up."

"That's enough," Chalmers said. "Did you find anything else in there?"

"Same as the other two, I'm afraid, Bob," Webber said. "No sign of a struggle – we pulled some prints but I'm not holding out much hope. This guy is good, I'll give him that."

"Did you get inside the locked room?"

"Locked room?" Webber said.

"Upstairs. There's a room that's locked. Why is it locked?"

"Hold on," Webber went upstairs.

He came back down a short while later and walked past without saying a word.

Webber came back inside the house carrying a crowbar.

"This should do the trick. Let's go and have a look."

It took him only a couple of seconds to get the door open. The lock snapped with a loud crack. The light was on inside the room and the window was covered by a thick, black curtain.

"Looks like some kind of office," Bridge observed. "That curtain is a bit excessive don't you think?"

"Black-out curtain," Chalmers said. "Maybe he liked to work away from daylight."

"Let's see what he was working on, shall we?" Webber approached the desk and flipped open the laptop.

"Screen saver," he said. "I wonder why he left it on."

He swiped a gloved finger over the pad and an image appeared on the screen.

"Have a look at this," he said to Bridge and Chalmers.

"Bloody hell," Bridge looked at the screen. "That looks like a school changing room."

"It's a video," Webber clicked the play icon.

The screen was filled with naked and half-naked schoolgirls.

"This bloke liked to watch schoolgirls," Bridge said.

"And this looks like an amateur video," Webber said. "Look at the girls – it's clear they have no idea they're been filmed."

"Hidden camera?" Chalmers speculated.

"Looks like it," Webber said and switched off the video.

He clicked on another file and waited for it to upload.

"Another one," he stared at the grainy image on the screen. "It looks like the same changing room, although the angle is different."

"Do you think he planted a camera in the girls' changing rooms?" Bridge asked. "Or did he get it off the web?"

"This is an MP4 file," Webber said.

He right-clicked and brought up the *properties*. "The file was created two weeks ago, and modified a week later. Last access was Friday last week. Look at the label."

"Kingfield Secondary19.3.18." Bridge read. "That's a school on the Hull Road. My God, he's been filming the girls' changing room at my old school."

CHAPTER THIRTY TWO

Smith was numb. Every inch of him felt numb. Whitton's reaction to his confession had unnerved him. He would have preferred it if she'd screamed or lashed out and hit him, but she'd sat calmly in the hospital bed and told him to leave.

"Leave," she said. "Leave now."

That was all. Smith had left the hospital and got into his car with no idea where he was going to go. He couldn't go back to work and he didn't feel like going back to a home that was no longer a home.

He'd lost everything in a matter of days. His job and his wife. Everything that was important was now gone.

He had nothing left.

He left the city behind and headed north. It was a drive he'd taken many times before. To a place where he could think and unravel the thoughts inside his head.

The Moors Centre in Danby was closed. It was another couple of weeks before the tourist season and Smith had the whole place to himself. He got out of the car and walked along the path towards the river. There had been very little rain recently and the Esk was low. Smith sat on the bank and gazed into the slowly-running stream.

One night, he thought, *one night and one stupid mistake and now years of trust have been broken*.

He knew that things between him and Whitton could never be the same again. He picked up a rock and threw it into the river. A hidden moorhen dashed across the water and took to the air in disgust.

Smith got up and started to walk towards the moors in the distance. He reached the highest point and stopped. He looked across the vast expanse of heather. He was all alone up here – there wasn't another soul in sight. He breathed in the fresh air and closed his eyes. An image of Whitton's face filled his head. Her expression changing when Smith told her about Baldwin. Her eyes had darkened and the sparkle that had been there a few moments before was gone. Smith would never be able to get that image out of his head.

It was late afternoon when Smith arrived back in York. He turned into his road and slowed down. Whitton's father's car was parked outside his house. As Smith got closer he could see that Whitton's mother and Laura were sitting in the back. Whitton and her father emerged from the house and Whitton locked the door. She was carrying a large suitcase. Smith got out of the car and approached them.

"We need to talk," he said to his wife.

Whitton ignored him, opened up the car boot and put the suitcase inside.

"Erica," Smith pleaded.

"Not now, son," Harold Whitton said.

"I just want to talk to her," Smith said.

"Not now," Harold said again and got in the car.

Smith watched as he started the engine and pulled away from the kerb. He stood outside for a long time gazing at the empty road that Harold Whitton had just driven away on.

He went inside the house and collapsed on the sofa in the living room. The dogs were still outside in the back garden and Smith didn't have the energy left in him to let them in.

What the hell have I done? Smith he thought. *Why do I always seem to destroy everything that's important?*

For once in his life everything was running along smoothly – he had a beautiful daughter, an amazing wife and a career that was finally on the way up.

But now he'd ruined it all.

He got off the sofa. He decided he would do what he always did when he needed to forget about the demons in his head.

* * *

Bridge was already seated when Smith walked inside the café. He'd suggested to Bridge that they meet somewhere discreet – somewhere nobody knew them. Bridge had been reluctant at first but eventually Smith persuaded him to give him half an hour of his time.

"Thanks for coming," Smith said and sat down. "Have you ordered yet?"

"I've only just got here myself," Bridge told him.

Smith managed to get the attention of a surly-looking waitress. She didn't look much older than a schoolgirl. She put down her mobile phone and ambled over to their table.

"Just two coffees please," Smith ordered.

She sighed and walked off, obviously annoyed about having to miss out on what was happening on her phone for the sake of two measly coffees.

"What do you want?" Bridge asked.

There was a bruise forming under his chin where Smith had punched him earlier. Smith unconsciously rubbed the spot where both Bridge and Smyth had hit him.

"That's going to be a bit sore," Smith pointed to the bruise. "Sorry again about that."

"Don't be," Bridge said. "I've had worse than this. You should see Smyth at the moment – he's going to have a real shiner in a day or two. No doubt he'll make up some Rambo story."

"Is he still pissed off?"

"I wouldn't know. What do you want?"

"I'm going crazy at home," Smith said. "Whitton is staying with her parents with Laura, and I can't just sit back and forget about the investigation."

"There's been another one. Another murder with the same MO. A perv was killed in his living room. The daughter found him this morning with both eyes gouged out and a knife sticking out of his heart. It's a similar knife to the others."

"My God," Smith said.

The waitress arrived with their coffee and slammed the tray down on the table so hard that the coffee spilled. She began to offload the milk and sugar with the same heavy hand.

"I'll do that," Smith offered. "It would be nice if there was some coffee left in the cups to drink."

"What?" the waitress was obviously not well-schooled in sarcasm.

"You get back to your social media," Smith added.

She turned around and did just that.

"Kids today are real miserable bastards," Smith said.

"You're just getting old," Bridge helped himself to four sugars. "You were like that not so long ago."

"Do we know much about the recent victim?" Smith asked.

"Alex Power," Bridge said. "He works as a plumber. The wife's away at some dental conference but she'll be back later today. We did find something interesting in the house though."

"Go on."

"One of the doors upstairs was locked, but Webber is quite handy with a crowbar and got it open in seconds. It looks like it was Power's office. It was really creepy – the windows were covered with these thick impenetrable curtains and he'd left his laptop on. There was some rather disturbing stuff on there."

"Underage porn?" Smith speculated.

"How did you know that?" Bridge was amazed.

"His eyes," Smith said. "You said his eyes were gouged out, so I assume this killer, this self-proclaimed God figure wanted to punish him for something he's looked at that he shouldn't have."

"There were a load of video files of the girls' changing rooms at my old school, Kingfield Secondary. Power somehow managed to get in there and install hidden cameras. It's not hardcore stuff, but it's still quite sick if you ask me. It looks like he was watching the videos and he was disturbed. His laptop was still switched on."

"Did you find his phone?"

"Same message as the others," Bridge said. "And I made sure Webber bagged it himself and held onto it."

"What are you talking about?"

"Webber's new guy managed to lose the other two phones somehow. The ones belonging to Peter Ashe and John Ware. He says he doesn't know what he did with them."

"You've got to be kidding me," Smith said. "That was vital evidence. Where the hell did Webber find this idiot?"

"He came highly recommended, and you know Webber wouldn't let just anybody onto his team."

"I have to get going," Bridge said and finished what was left in his cup. "Chalmers has called a briefing and I'm only going to make it by the skin of my teeth as it is. What are you going to do?"

"I need you to do me a favour."

"Of course you do."

"Find out if the latest victim was religious. Find out if he went to church. More precisely, find out if he was part of the St Olave congregation. I assume this is just an initial briefing?"

"It is. We've spoken to the daughter, but the wife isn't due back until later, so we don't know very much about the bloke yet."

"Besides being a sicko who liked to film teenage girls?"

"Besides that. I still don't know what's going on here. Three dead men. All of them with body parts removed."

"I think it's pretty clear," Smith said. "Keep me in the loop."

CHAPTER THIRTY THREE

Smith parked his car illegally as close to St Olave's Church as possible. He wound up the windows and opened the door. He'd decided to do some snooping around on his own. Father Jacob Swift was talking to a woman on the steps. She had her back to Smith and he couldn't see her face. Smith stayed in the car and watched. From the proximity to one another and the way Father Swift was resting his hand on the woman's shoulder it was clear that they knew each other. They finished their conversation and the woman turned around. She had metal studs and rings all over her face. It was Penelope Slyper, Heidi Ashe's sister.

Smith got out of the car and approached her. She didn't appear to notice him at first, but when she did her facial expression changed immediately. It wasn't disdain on her face now, it was something else. Smith was sure she appeared embarrassed to see him.

"Good afternoon," he said to her.

"What are you doing here?" she asked.

"I just needed to speak to Father Swift. He and I are becoming good friends. What about you, what are *you* doing here?"

"Not that it's any of your business, but someone has to arrange the funeral. That's if you lot decide to release Peter's body sometime this year."

"I'm very sorry about that," Smith said. "But it's usual in a murder investigation. Look at it this way – you wouldn't want to put your sister through the trauma of having her husband's body dug up later when some new evidence came to light, would you?"

"Heidi asked me to come," Penelope added. "She wasn't feeling up to it. Peter was a bastard, but he was still my sister's husband and this is what he would have wanted. I was just making some preliminary arrangements.

When do you believe my sister will be able to be able to bury her husband? When will she be allowed to begin mourning?"

"When we're finished," Smith replied rather bluntly.

He found Father Swift in his office again. He was typing something on his laptop. The door was open.

Smith knocked. "Sorry to bother you again. Would you mind if I speak to you?"

Father Swift looked up from the screen. "Of course. The door to St Olave's is always open. Come in and take a seat."

Smith sat opposite him at the desk. Father Swift minimized the email he was composing and looked at Smith.

"I assume this isn't a religious matter?"

"Religion and me have never really seen eye to eye," Smith admitted.

"What can I do for you then?"

"Do you know a man by the name of Alex Power?"

"Alex, yes. I do know him. Why do you ask?"

"Is he a member of your congregation?"

"He is. What's going on?"

"He's dead," Smith told him. "He was murdered. When was the last time you saw him? Did Mr Power happen to confess to something recently?"

"You know my stance where confession is concerned."

"And you know mine where the law is concerned. Please, Father Swift. This is extremely important. You don't need to go into details – I have a pretty good idea anyway. Has Alex Power been to confession recently?"

Father Swift rubbed his eyes and sighed. "He has."

"When was this?"

"Yesterday. Just after I spoke to you as a matter of fact."

"But that was quite late," Smith remembered. It was past eight in the evening when he'd spoken to Father Swift. "This really is an open-all-hours church, isn't it?"

"And that's all I'm going to say on the matter," Father Swift insisted. "Use your law if you have to, but confession is sacred. I'll go to prison before I break that sanctity."

"I understand," Smith said even though he didn't. "Can I tell you what Mr Power confessed to? You can correct me if I'm wrong, but I already know that Mr Power liked to watch schoolgirls. In fact he even went so far as to install a hidden camera in the girls' changing rooms at one of the local schools so he could watch them coming out of the showers. Naked."

Father Swift's facial expression didn't change.

"Am I getting warm?" Smith asked.

"I cannot answer that."

"OK, let me ask you something else. Do you forgive these penitents? Is it as simple as that?"

"Only God can make that choice," Father Swift said. "It is He who decides on forgiveness. I am merely here to offer direction. It is up to the individual to choose the path they wish to take."

"I see," Smith had thought of something Bridge told him earlier. "Alex Power came here to confess at around eight yesterday evening. We both know what he wanted to get off his chest. You listened and then told him to make his own choices. Is that about right?"

"It goes much deeper than that, but that's about right."

"And what if I told you that Mr Power went straight home from the confessional booth, switched on his computer and carried on where he left off before the confession? Not long after he sought forgiveness for his sins he was right back where he started. Ogling naked schoolgirls on a hidden camera."

"I have nothing further to say to you," Father Swift said. "I think it's time for you to leave."

"How do you know Penelope Slyper?" Smith changed the subject.

"Penny helps out around here sometimes," Father Swift replied. "What has that got to do with anything?"

"Helps out?"

"She has a kind heart, and she believes in doing good. Always. The good man will be rewarded and the sinner, punished. It is her way of life."

"Karma?"

"Some call it that."

"Eastern Philosophy?" Smith suggested. "Forgive my ignorance, but isn't that against Christian belief?"

"I'm not going to enter into a debate about religion here, detective – we would be here all night, but what I will explain is how religion has changed. We simply don't get the feet we used to if you'll pardon my crudeness. If a member of my congregation chooses to believe in Buddhism, Hinduism, I do not have a problem with it. If they are following the right path in their beliefs then we're all striving for the same thing, aren't we?"

"Which is?"

"Loving thy fellow man."

Amen to that, Smith thought but managed to hold his tongue.

"One last question," he said. "What exactly does Penelope Slyper do here? You said she helps out occasionally."

"She helps me with the admin and she's even been known to do a bit of cleaning from time to time. Penny is a very kind-hearted woman. Her appearance invites undeserved judgment, but who are we to judge?"

"Who are we to judge?" Smith mused. "I'll leave you in peace. Thank you for your time. I'll make sure you're informed as to when Peter Ashe's body will be released."

"Excuse me?" Father Swift frowned.

"For the funeral," Smith elaborated. "That's what Miss Slyper was doing here, wasn't it? Arranging things for the funeral?"

"She didn't mention it to me."

"So, she wasn't here to talk about Peter Ashe's funeral?"

"I'm sure Mrs Ashe will speak to me in due course about that. Good afternoon, detective."

CHAPTER THIRTY FOUR

"Look at us," DCI Chalmers glanced around the room.

He, Bridge, Yang Chu and Baldwin sat in the small conference room.

"This room is so empty I swear there's an echo in here," Chalmers continued. "If this is the future of a murder investigation team then I think it's time I thought about early retirement."

"Where's Smith?" Baldwin asked.

"Compassionate leave," Chalmers replied. "Among other things. Let's get a move on, shall we?"

Baldwin blushed.

Grant Webber came in with his assistant, Harry. They sat down without saying anything.

"Now it's looking more like a full team," Chalmers said. "Alex Power. What do we know about the man?"

"Thirty-eight-years-old," Bridge replied. "Married with a sixteen-year-old daughter. He's a self-employed plumber."

"He must do alright then," Yang Chu said. "Plumbers know how to charge."

"Let's not waste time here," Chalmers said. "Anything else?"

"We've spoken to his daughter, Sophie," Bridge said. "She was the one who found him, but we haven't had chance to talk to his wife. She's on her way back from a conference in Wales as we speak."

"I'll go over what we do know," Chalmers said. "Alex Power was found at around half-ten this morning by his daughter. He was lying on the sofa in his living room with a knife in his chest. Both of his eyes were gouged out, and, as we didn't find the eyes at the scene we can assume the murderer took them with him. There was a message on his phone which turns out to be the same message as the ones sent to Peter Ashe and John Ware shortly after they were killed. This is the same killer without a doubt. Grant? Do you have anything to add?"

"As you're probably aware," the Head of Forensics began. "Two pieces of what may have been vital evidence were misplaced."

Yang Chu snorted. "Misplaced?"

"That is correct," Webber said. "But those mobile phones have since been recovered. Unfortunately neither of them yielded anything."

"What about the number the messages were sent from?" Bridge asked.

"Different numbers," Webber said. "Both pre-paid and neither of them are in service anymore so it's safe to assume whoever sent those messages dumped the sims straight afterwards. We made Alex Power's mobile phone a priority and found the same thing. Those sim cards are no longer on the network."

"Damn it," Yang Chu cursed. "I was sure they would give us some kind of breakthrough."

"We can't be sure if Mr Power was drugged before he was killed and his eyes were removed – pathology is still busy, but for his sake I hope that he was. My opinion is he was still alive when his eyes were gouged out, and it was the stab wound to his heart that killed him."

"Motive," Chalmers said out of the blue. "Motive, motive, bloody motive. Does anyone have any theories?"

Silence.

"Anybody?" Chalmers urged.

"As far as we're aware," Bridge said. "These men didn't know each other, and we haven't come up with a single thread that can link them together. No mutual acquaintances, no work ties, nothing. So that would suggest this isn't a revenge thing. This isn't the work of a maniac who believes he's been wronged, and has to make amends."

"What *does* it suggest?" Chalmers asked.

"I think we're dealing with a psychopath," Bridge said.

"A very intelligent one," Webber added.

"There's no research to suggest that intelligence and madness are mutually exclusive," Yang Chu joined in. "Quite the opposite in fact – many documented serial killers were of above average intelligence."

"I reckon we should work on some kind of profile," Bridge suggested.

"Let's leave the FBI bollocks for when we really get desperate," Chalmers said. "Right, we've exhausted the motive part, what about opportunity? All of these murders have one thing in common – they were definitely not spur of the moment acts. These were carefully planned and meticulously carried out. Peter Ashe was separated from his wife and was alone at home. John Ware also lived alone. Alex Power's wife was away at a conference and his daughter was staying with a friend."

"Do you think they were being watched?" Baldwin said.

"It is possible. How else would the killer be sure not to be disturbed? Let's take a short break and refuel with some coffee. I know it's getting late, but tough shit – we've still got a lot to go through."

Twenty minutes later, they reconvened. The coffee didn't appear to have worked. The red eyes and the desperate faces on the investigation team indicated the exhaustion they were all feeling.

"Where were we?" Chalmers said.

"You said something about them being watched," Bridge reminded him.

"It's a theory we need to look into. Let's look more closely at the most recent murder."

"Alex Power," Bridge said.

The briefing was turning into the Chalmers-Bridge show.

"His eyes were gouged out," Bridge said. "And we suspect what we found on his computer may have something to do with that. Mr Power liked to spy on teenage girls. Especially naked ones."

"You're kidding?" This was clearly news to Baldwin.

"It appears he hooked up some kind of hidden camera in the girls' changing rooms at Kingfield Secondary School. It's my old school. We found a load of videos on his computer."

"How did he manage to get in there in the first place?" Baldwin asked. "Schools are quite secure these days – you can't just walk in and plant a camera, especially not in the changing rooms."

"His daughter mentioned something about him doing some plumbing work at a school," Chalmers remembered. "I think that's how he gained access. He could have quite easily stuck the camera up while he was working. We'll check to see which school he was working at, but I'll bet a week's wages it was Kingfield."

"What a sicko," Baldwin pulled a face. "Those poor girls weren't even aware they were being filmed."

"So," Chalmers said. "We've got a bloke who was having an affair with a fourteen-year-old, a known thief and a man who liked to spy on naked schoolgirls. None of these men are what you would call upstanding citizens. The philanderer had his tackle lopped off - the thief died minus his hands and the hidden camera expert was blind when he entered the wide beyond."

"The punishment fits the crime?" Bridge suggested.

"But who is the punisher?" Chalmers said. "Who believes it is his God-given right to dole out these punishments?"

Everyone in the room smelled it at almost exactly the same time. Alcohol.

It was stuffy in the small conference room, so the door was left open. The alcohol fumes became more noticeable. Smith staggered in and sat down next to Chalmers.

"Sorry to barge in, but I think I may have stumbled upon something important."

CHAPTER THIRTY FIVE

"You're pissed," Chalmers wrinkled his nose. "Go home and sleep it off."

"I'm not pissed," Smith articulated every word. "I had a couple of beers, that's all. Maybe three. I haven't eaten anything, and the beer has gone straight to my head."

"If Smyth finds you in here you'll be sacked on the spot," Chalmers added.

"Boss," Smith looked at him through bloodshot eyes. "I really couldn't give a fuck. My wife has left me. She's taken my child with her. There's nothing that public-school faggot can do to me that will make me feel any worse. Do you want to know what I have to say or not?"

"Make it quick," Chalmers said.

Smith looked around the room. Bridge, Yang Chu, Webber and Harry looked at him with open mouths. Only Baldwin avoided his gaze.

"I'll make it quick," Smith said. "All three murders lead back to St Olave's Church. It's as simple as that."

"What makes you think that?" Chalmers asked.

"Peter Ashe confessed to something shortly before he was killed. As did John Ware. And I recently found out that Alex Power was not long out of the confessional both at St Olave's before he too, had his expiry date brought forward."

"How did you know about Power?" Chalmers asked.

"I heard about it," Smith said. "It's not important. I spoke to Father Swift earlier and he told me that Alex Power came to see him around eight yesterday evening. What time was his body found?"

"His daughter found him at half-ten this morning," Yang Chu said.

"No TOD yet?"

"I'd say he'd been dead for a good few hours when we got there," Grant Webber speculated.

"So, you see why you need to concentrate on the church then?" Smith said. "Mr Power confesses to something then he's killed. I couldn't get any more details out of Father Swift as to the nature of the confession, but he neither confirmed nor denied it had something to do with young girls."

Smith was somewhat animated, but he appeared to have sobered up in an instant. His words were clear and his thinking, rational.

"What are you suggesting?" Bridge said. "That we go and raid a church?"

"Yes, that's what I'm suggesting."

"And what exactly are we looking for?"

"Use your head. Men are being killed after confessing. The confession is between the confessor, Father Swift and God. Nobody else is privy to what is said in that booth."

"Do you think Father Swift had something to do with this?" Chalmers said.

"Inadvertently, yes, although I don't think he's the one who killed those men."

"You've lost me there," Yang Chu admitted. "If these murders have something to do with these men's confessions and only Father Swift and God have heard what was said, who are you suggesting we look at, God?"

Smith let out a quiet belch. "I'll admit, I haven't got that far yet. There's something Ungodly about that church, you mark my words."

He stood up and swayed from one side to the other. Then he seemed to gather his composure and walked out of the room.

Nobody spoke for a while. Smith's fleeting visit seemed to have taken everyone by surprise. The smell of stale beer still lingered in the air.

"He could be onto something," Bridge was the first to break the silence. "About the confessions I mean. I think we need to bring Father Swift in for questioning."

"He's a Vicar," Baldwin reminded him.

"And the last time I checked; Vicars were not above the law." He looked at Chalmers. "What do you think, sir?"

"Bridge is right," Chalmers said. "And I hate to admit it, but so is Smith. Pissed or not, he made some valid points back there. It's getting late but we'll see what our Father Swift has to tell us first thing in the morning."

* * *

Father Jacob Swift shut down his computer and was about to switch off the light in his office when he heard a noise coming from the main body of the church. He left the light on and went to see what was going on. The interior of the church was dimly lit as it always was at night and Father Swift had to wait a while for his eyes to become accustomed to the softer lighting after the bright fluorescent glow of his office. He heard the sound again – a quiet scraping sound. It sounded like it was coming from the area around the confessional booth.

"Hello," he shouted. "Is someone there?"

The words echoed off the walls in the empty church.

"Hello," he tried again.

Nothing.

St Olave's had suffered from a rat problem a few years earlier. A team of exterminators had been brought in and the rats hadn't returned.

Maybe they're back, Father Swift thought. *Maybe it was the sound of a rat's feet I head.*

The church was now silent. Father Swift could hear the low hum of the fluorescent light in his office. He went back and flicked the switch.

He heard the noise again, and this time he knew for certain that it was not a rat. It was the sound of footsteps walking on wooden floors.

"Who's there?" he tried to make his voice sound deeper but it didn't work. The words came out as a fearful croak.

"I can't help you if you don't show yourself."

Father Swift now felt very afraid. He didn't know what it was but his whole body was becoming filled with dread. There was something sinister about the noises in the church.

Or the absence of sound.

That was even worse. There were no more footsteps, and the scraping sound had stopped. Father Swift breathed in deeply to try and slow his heartbeat, and made his way towards the entrance of the church.

It started as a slight burning sensation on his back and then an inferno began to blaze inside his chest. Father Swift tried to call out, but all he could manage were a few guttural gasps. He pressed his hand over his chest and sliced open his palm. Something sharp was sticking out of his chest. He didn't have time to figure out what it was. His heart fought to keep going, but then it stopped pumping for good and Father Swift fell face-forward next to the confessional booth.

The woman was waiting outside St Olave's Church. She was breathing heavily and the way her lip was quivering suggested a sobbing episode wasn't far away.

"Get a grip," the man said and stared at her. "It's done. It had to be done. We still have work to do."

CHAPTER THIRTY SIX

Smith was debating whether to open another beer or go straight to bed when he heard the sound of a car door closing outside in the street. Shortly afterwards somebody rang his doorbell. Smith's mind was made up. He took a beer out of the fridge and went to answer the door.

Yang Chu was standing outside. "Are you busy?"

"What do you want?" Smith asked.

"I was in the area and I thought I'd pop in and say hello."

"Bullshit. Come in. Do you want a beer?"

"Might as well," Yang Chu replied and went inside.

"I'm going out for a smoke," Smith opened up the back door. "The beers are in the fridge."

He sat on the bench in the back garden. Yang Chu sat opposite him.

Smith held up his beer. "Cheers."

Yang Chu raised his. "I just wanted to give you a heads-up, Sarge. Everybody knows."

"Don't be vague," Smith told him. "Everybody knows what?"

"About you and Baldwin."

Smith didn't seem surprised. "It was bound to come out sooner or later. How did they find out so quickly?"

"Bridge asked the DCI right after you left the briefing. The cheeky bastard came right out and asked him what was really going on with you."

"I expected more from Chalmers," Smith took a long swig of his beer.

"It wasn't the DCI," Yang Chu said. "Chalmers is old-school and he's the sort who will take a secret to the grave if he has to. It was Baldwin."

"Baldwin?" Smith almost choked on his beer.

"She spoke up and said she might as well tell the team before the speculation started. Apparently, Whitton phoned her earlier and told her she's welcome to you. I'm sorry, Sarge."

"So am I," Smith sighed. "And there's one thing that dulls the ache that being sorry causes and that's beer. Can I get you another?"

"I wouldn't say no. it's been a rough few days."

"I'll drink to that."

Smith returned with two more beers and lit a cigarette.

"So what now then, Sarge?" Yang Chu said.

"We drink until there's no more left," Smith demonstrated his intentions by finishing half of the bottle in one impressive gulp.

"I mean you and Whitton. Surely there's a way for you to patch things up."

"I don't think this can be patched up," Smith said. "I think things have gone far beyond the patching-up stage."

"How did Whitton find out?"

"I told her. I couldn't handle the guilt so I told her. Not one of my brightest ideas."

"It could have been worse," Yang Chu said. "It would have been worse if she'd found out from someone else, or caught you at it."

"It was a one off," Smith glared at him. "It happened once. What is this? What's with all the Agony Aunt advice? Are you thinking of changing careers and offering advice in magazines?"

"I'm worried about you, Sarge," Yang Chu ignored him. "And I'm worried about Whitton. In case you've forgotten, we happen to go back a long way."

"I don't need anyone's pity. I cheated on my wife and shagged another woman. I couldn't keep my dick in my pants, and I slept with a colleague from work. Now unless you want to change the subject, you can fuck off right now."

Yang Chu gazed up at the dark clouds forming overhead. "Looks like rain."

Smith finished the rest of his beer then burst out laughing. He slapped Yang Chu on the shoulder. Then he slapped him again.

"Easy," Yang Chu said. "You may have given the Super and Bridge a bit of a hiding but you won't find it so easy with me."

"You reckon?"

"Give it a go. I'll knock you on your arse in seconds."

Smith knew Yang Chu was right. He didn't stand a chance against him.

"Thanks, mate," Smith said. "I promise I won't try and knock you out. Thanks for coming round. I appreciate it."

"I think I preferred it when you were agro. Chalmers has agreed to bring Father Swift in for questioning tomorrow morning."

"That should be interesting. Try and keep it away from the press for as long as possible. That lot will have a field day if they get wind of it."

"Do you think he knows something about all of this?"

"I'm sure he does. And maybe a good old-fashioned police interrogation will be enough to make him change his mind about his sacred confessional beliefs. We're not in the Middle Ages anymore."

A rumble of thunder was heard overhead. It sounded like it was still some way off in the distance.

"I told you it was going to rain," Yang Chu said. "When are you coming back to work?"

"Chalmers told me to piss off for a few days," Smith told him. "Which, by my standards is quite a brief suspension. He just wanted to give Smyth a while to cool down a bit."

"You should see his face. He's got quite a shiner and the funny part is, the moron seems proud of it. He's parading around with his head held high showing off his black eye to everyone who'll look at it. I don't think he's ever had one before."

"I doubt that. He went to a public-school remember."

The thunder was louder now and flashes of lightning lit up the sky around them.

"I'd better get home before the storm really gets going," Yang Chu said and drained what was left in his bottle. "Thanks for the beer. I'll keep you up to speed with what's happening in the investigation."

"Cheers," Smith raised his glass and lifted it to his lips but it was empty.

"Another one bites the dust. You OK to see yourself out?"

Yang Chu smiled and walked back inside the house.

* * *

An hour or so later the storm hit the City of York with a vengeance. Thunder and lightning boomed and flashed almost continuously and then the rain came. What began as a light pitter-patter onto the pavement and rooftops culminated in a torrential downpour. Within seconds rivers of water were gushing through the streets and alleyways. The roads around Marygate were now rivers. Two men in their late teens were unlucky enough to be walking home from a party in Bootham when the worst of the storm hit. They were halfway along Marygate when the heavens opened.

"Holy Shit," Jack Johnson exclaimed. "It's pissing it down."

"And the award for stating the bloody obvious goes to..." his friend, Ian Tyler laughed.

Within seconds they were both drenched.

"Let's see if we can find some shelter," Jack suggested. "I'm soaked."

"What's the point?" Ian asked. "There comes a point where it's impossible to become any wetter. Saturation point I think it's called."

"Will you stop with your intellectual nonsense? You're a temp in a library, not a rocket scientist. Look, across the road – it looks like the lights in the church are on. They have to give us shelter in a church don't they?"

"You're so beautifully misinformed, my friend. Firstly, this is the twenty-first century and the church will be locked, and probably armed with a security system to rival Fort Knox. And, secondly, since when did the church give a hoot about helping people?"

"The lights are on," Jack ignored him. "At least it will be dry in there."

Ian reluctantly followed him up the steps towards the entrance of St Olave's. The door was wide open.

"See," Jack screamed. "I told you, the doors are always open in a church."

They went inside the shelter of the church. The noise of the rain pelting down on the roof was horrendous.

"I think I've gone deaf," Ian bellowed.

"What?" Jack couldn't hear him over the din of the rain.

He took off his jacket and shook his head. Droplets of rain flew in all directions. The noise on the roof appeared to be getting louder – the storm was showing no sign of letting up.

"Let's have a look around," Ian suggested.

Jack hadn't yet learned how to lip-read so his friend's words went unanswered. Ian walked a few paces and stopped. He looked up at the stained-glass windows. Once in a while the images on them were emphasised by the flashes of lightning outside. Ian was mesmerised. The spectacle was hypnotic. He didn't notice that Jack had joined him and they both gazed up at the light show above them.

The rain was definitely easing off now. And the thunder was becoming more intermittent.

"It's moving off," Jack said. "I reckon we'll be able to walk home in a few minutes."

"I've never been inside this church before," Ian said. "It's quite cool with the storm outside. Do you think we..."

"What the hell is that?" Jack interrupted the question he was about to ask.

"What?"

"Over there," Jack pointed to something on the floor by the confessional booth.

"What is that?"

"That's what I just said."

Jack moved cautiously towards the mystery object on the floor. The dim light inside the church seemed to be playing tricks with his eyes. First, the object resembled a bundle of rags, then, as he got nearer, and he saw the handle of the Kila dagger sticking out, he really couldn't imagine what he was looking at."

"It looks like someone left a whole pile of clothes here," Ian said.

Father Swift's head was hidden from view by one side of the confessional booth. All the two men could see at that moment was a large coat and a pair of trousers. They moved closer. It was Jack who saw it first.

"Oh my God. It's a bloke."

Ian walked around him to get a better look. Father Swift was lying on his stomach. His head was twisted to the side and his eyes were wide open. Ian turned away and vomited against the side of the confessional booth. Then both young men ran. They ran out of the church and then they ran the whole length of Marygate.

CHAPTER THIRTY SEVEN

PC Hugo Limpet was manning the switchboard when the call came in an hour later. PC Limpet had recently transferred to York from Leeds. He'd transferred to Leeds from Halifax and before that he'd worked in Bradford. Limpet wasn't a name that had done Hugo any favours in the police. It wasn't a name that would ensure his rapid ascent up the ranks. That's just the way it was.

His joke of a name aside, Hugo was very good at his job. He was diligent, intelligent and extremely conscientious and when the hysterical voice on the other end of the phone screamed something Hugo couldn't understand he calmly told the caller to take a deep breath and repeat what he'd just said more slowly. It seemed to do the trick. Within ten minutes, two police cars were parked outside St Olave's Church on Marygate. DC Yang Chu had also been informed and was en route. PC Limpet hadn't been able to contact DS Bridge.

The downpour from earlier that night meant the roads were treacherous. Yang Chu didn't like driving at thirty miles per hour – his Ford Focus wasn't designed to go so slowly, but the pools of water on the tarmac meant he had no choice. He made it to the church without incident and stopped the car outside. He looked at the clock on the dashboard and sighed. It was almost three in the morning. He was thankful he'd only had two beers at Smith's house – he was surely well under the limit, but the lack of sleep meant he was probably going to feel even more exhausted by the end of the day than he did yesterday.

"What have we got?" Yang Chu asked the PC manning the entrance of the church.

"Dead body," the PC replied. "Two teenagers on their way home from a party got caught in the storm and took shelter in the church. They ran home and called it in."

"Thanks," Yang Chu said and yawned a gaping yawn.

He didn't even try and hide it.

Another two uniformed officers were standing inside the church. Yang Chu wondered what they were actually there for – he hadn't seen a soul on the streets as he drove here, and the earlier storm would surely mean nobody would be out at this time in the morning.

"Where is it?" he asked the taller of the two.

"Over there by the confessional booth. Looks like he's been stabbed in the back. Can you believe it – stabbed in the back in a church? That's irony for you, don't you think?"

"No," Yang Chu said and walked up to the confessional booth.

Father Jacob Swift had now been dead for a good few hours and his features had altered dramatically since the Kila knife had stopped his heart. His eyes were bulging, and his skin was now a light bluish-black colour. Very soon rigor mortis would begin, and it would become more difficult to manoeuvre his limbs. Yang Chu had never met Father Swift before so he didn't know if the man lying inside the church with a knife sticking out of his back was Swift or not. For all he knew the body could have been brought here after he was killed, and the position of the body next to the confessional booth made him believe that was the case. He didn't want to check for ID until forensics had arrived.

He went back outside. The scent of the recent downpour was still in the air even though the sky was now clear and stars were visible for the first time that night. Nobody else had arrived at the scene yet. It was just Yang Chu, and the three PC's.

"Have forensics been informed?" he asked the PC manning the entrance.

"I think so," the PC replied.

"You think so? What the hell?"

He took out his phone and called the switchboard.

"York Police. PC Limpet speaking. How may I assist you?"

"Limpet," Yang Chu said. "Have forensics been made aware of the dead body here at St Olave's Church?"

"Of course. I followed procedure. Uniform to seal off the scene then forensics. And you lot in CID of course. Do you want me to see if there's some kind of problem?"

"Thanks, that won't be necessary. I'll give Webber a call on his mobile."

"Right you are."

Yang Chu brought up Webber's number. The Head of Forensics picked up straight away.

"Don't you ever sleep?" Yang Chu said.

"Not much," Webber said. "What's the urgency? It's three in the morning."

"Didn't you get the word from the switchboard? A man's been found dead inside St Olave's. And if I'm not mistaken he was stabbed with one of those monk daggers."

"Nobody contacted me," Webber said. "St Olave's you say?"

"That's right."

"I'll be there in twenty minutes."

He rang off.

A black car stopped behind Yang Chu's Ford Focus. Yang Chu didn't recognise it. The door opened and, Harry, Webber's technician got out.

"I got here as soon as I could," he told Yang Chu. "You take your life in your hands driving on these roads after a downpour like that."

"Why wasn't Webber informed?" Yang Chu asked.

"Let me tell you something, constable. I am not some trainee forensics technician fresh out of school – I happen to have worked with some of the busiest departments in the country. I personally requested this transfer, and the dip in salary that accompanied it so I could get to work side-by-side with Grant Webber. I am more than capable of handling a crime scene. Now, if you have no further questions I'd appreciate it if you could just stay out of my way and let me do my job."

It was Yang Chu's weariness that stopped him from knocking this jumped-up forensics officer to the ground. Had he felt more awake he dreaded to think what he might have done. He watched as Harry grabbed his bag from the car and went inside the church. Yang Chu didn't like him one little bit. Without knowing why, he followed him inside.

Harry had told the two PC's to leave him in peace and they now stood with the third PC by the entrance. Yang Chu ducked to one side behind one of the pews. He watched Webber's technician go through the motions. Harry opened up his bag and laid it on the floor next to him. Yang Chu noticed he wasn't wearing the usual Scene of Crime suit. Harry stood up and looked around the church and for a moment Yang Chu wondered if his presence had been discovered.

Harry carried on working. Yang Chu watched as he shone a torch onto Father Swift and pulled the knife out in one swift motion. He wasn't wearing gloves. He set the knife down and rolled Father Swift over. He then reached inside the inside pocket of the jacket and rummaged around. The light inside the church meant Yang Chu couldn't get a clear picture of what was happening. Finally, Harry straightened up and Yang Chu saw him place something in a clear plastic bag. Then he did something that made Yang Chu gasp. He rubbed his head. He rubbed it so hard that surely strands of hair and particles of his skin would land on the dead man. He ran his hands up and down his jacket and got to his feet.

Yang Chu did the same. He walked out into the aisle so that Harry would be able to see him.

"Almost done," Harry said.

"So I saw," Yang Chu said.

"What's that supposed to mean?"

"You know exactly what it's supposed to mean. I was here the whole time, and I've never seen an initial forensic like that before. I'll be sure to mention your conventional methods to your boss. He should be here in a couple of minutes."

Harry's eyes widened. Yang Chu nodded and walked back outside.

CHAPTER THIRTY EIGHT

Smith was woken up by a dog licking his face. It took him a moment to realise it wasn't Theakston's slobbering tongue but the much shorter, more delicate one of Fred, the unsightly Pug. Fred's breath stank but Smith smiled.

"Good morning to you, too. What time is it?"

The Pug didn't reply but Smith saw from the clock on the bedside table that it was almost eight. Smith patted the bed next to him and his smile faded. He remembered that Whitton had left him. She'd left him and taken Laura with her. The pit of his stomach felt empty and it wasn't just because he hadn't eaten anything in a very long time. He got up and went downstairs.

After letting the dogs out he made some coffee and sat at the table in the kitchen with his head in his hands. The house was too quiet. Normally, Laura would be eating her breakfast at the table. His daughter would be devouring anything that was put in front of her. Whitton would be making her usual comments about how much a three-year-old could put away, and Smith would be smiling contentedly at the whole scene.

But not this morning.

This morning felt like he was living the life of somebody else. It was a life he hoped he would never have to live again. Waking up alone and going to bed alone. The Bull Terrier and the Pug were something but they weren't enough. The sound of the doorbell snapped Smith out of his temporary depression. He went to see who it was.

For the second time in only a few hours, Yang Chu stood outside Smith's house. He looked exhausted.

"What is it this time?" Smith asked him. "People are going to start talking."

"Something's happened," Yang Chu said. "I thought you should know, and you've got much better coffee than I've got at home."

Smith stepped aside and Yang Chu came inside the house. He followed Smith through to the kitchen. Smith switched on the kettle to make some more coffee.

"What's happened?"

"Father Swift is dead," Yang Chu said. "I got a call in the early hours of the morning to go to St Olave's Church. Two teenagers found a body when they were sheltering from the rain. I didn't know who it was at first – I've never met the bloke, but Webber's technician found his driving licence in his pocket. It was Father Swift."

"Shit," Smith said. "That means we're back to square one. I was sure Father Swift would be able to give us some answers."

"There's more, Sarge, it looks like he was killed with one of those Tibetan daggers. He was stabbed in the back."

"Was there a message on his phone?"

"No, but there was something inside his pocket. It was a note."

"Are you going to keep me in suspense all day?" Smith said. "What did the note say?"

Yang Chu took out his notebook. "I copied it. It said:

The path of the righteous man is beset on all sides by the inequities of the selfish and the tyranny of evil men.

These are the demons of humanity, and I have taken them from you.

Go now for you are now free.

"What the hell does that mean?" Smith said.

"God knows," Yang Chu replied. "Some religious gobbledygook. We'll get someone who knows about that kind of thing to look into it."

Smith ran his finger around the rim of his coffee cup. "Why would someone kill Father Swift? It doesn't make any sense. The other three were understandable – they were men who had sinned in the Biblical sense. All Father Swift did was listen to their confessions."

"Maybe he had a few skeletons in his own closet," Yang Chu suggested.

"I met the man a few times," Smith said. "And I actually got to like him. I got a good feeling about him if you know what I mean. No, this was about something else."

"Like what?"

"There's only one thing I can think of. The murderer somehow realised we were getting closer to him through Father Swift and they acted before he could tell us anything."

"That's a bit far-fetched isn't it?"

"Is it? Think about it – this killer murders his victims shortly after they've confessed something to Father Swift. How did they know about the confessions and how did they manage to kill these men in such a short space of time? I'm going outside for a cigarette."

"Have you heard from Whitton?" Yang Chu asked.

"I haven't spoken to her since I told her about what happened with Baldwin," Smith said. "I want to speak to her – I need to speak to her, but I think maybe I should give her some time. I fucked up and it's going to be a long road back to what we had but I'm not giving up."

"You'll get there, Sarge," Yang Chu said. "You and Whitton belong together. It's as simple as that."

"Haven't you got a job to go to?"

"There was something else that was bothering me, Sarge."

"God, you're full of happy information this morning, aren't you?"

"Webber's new technician," Yang Chu said. "What do you know about him?"

"Nothing," Smith admitted. "But Grant Webber is no fool and he wouldn't hire just anybody. What's this all about?"

"I don't like him. I get the feeling there's something not quite right about him."

"The curse of the detective," Smith exhaled a huge cloud of smoke.

"It's more than that. And early this morning at the church, he did something that freaked me out."

"I'm listening."

"Webber wasn't even informed about the body," Yang Chu said. "This Harry bloke turned up on his own and took over the crime scene."

"Webber probably gave him the green light to do so."

"He didn't. I phoned Webber and he didn't know anything about it. Switchboard got through to forensics, Harry somehow got the call and he didn't even bother to let Webber know what was going on."

"You know what it's like when you're the new kid," Smith said. "You want to impress, and Harry probably thought he'd impress Webber by doing a good job with a crime scene."

"That's my point, Sarge, he didn't. He didn't do a good job. He made a total balls-up of it in my opinion. What kind of forensics technician approaches a crime scene wearing neither a SOC suit or gloves?"

"Are you sure?"

"I watched the whole thing," Yang Chu said. "He didn't know I was watching. He made sure that uniform were somewhere else and he got to work on his own. Not only did he pull the knife out with his bare hands he got his own hair and God-knows whatever other traces of himself all over the body."

"Hmm," Smith stubbed his cigarette out. "Sounds like he was a bit too keen and he got ahead of himself."

"I was there, Sarge," Yang Chu said. "It was really weird. It was as though he was purposefully trying to contaminate evidence."

CHAPTER THIRTY NINE

Smith parked his car outside Whitton's parent's house and sat for a while. He knew it was probably too soon to try and speak to her, but he couldn't sit at home all day moping about what his wife was thinking. He decided it would be better for Whitton to scream at him, tell him she hates him, than to mope and speculate on his own. He took a number of deep breaths in quick succession and got out of the car.

Harold Whitton answered the door with a grim expression on his face. It was not an angry look but more one that expressed disappointment. "Harold," Smith said. "I didn't know what else to do. I've messed up, and I don't know what to do to make it right. Please can I speak to Erica?" "I don't think she wants to talk to you, son," Harold told him. "She's still very upset."

"Please," Smith said. "If she tells me to go to hell I'll go. I just need to talk to her."

"She'll probably tell you more than that, lad. You'd better come in."

Smith followed him inside the house. He felt sick. He'd come face to face with murderers, psychopaths and all manner of depraved individuals before but the feeling he had in the pit of his stomach right now was far worse than he'd ever had in the company of those low lifes of society. Harold led him to the kitchen. Laura was sitting in her chair, eating as usual. Her face lit up when she saw Smith.

"Daddy."

Smith's face felt numb. He had to fight back the tears that were threatening to burst from his eyes.

"Hey, baby girl," he bent over and kissed Laura on the top of her head, lingering there to take in her scent.

Jane Whitton came in. "What's he doing here?" she asked Harold without even acknowledging Smith.

"He's come to try and make amends," Harold told her.

"I'd say it's too late for that, wouldn't you?"

"Mrs Whitton," Smith decided on a more formal approach. "Please. I know what I did was terrible."

"Unforgivable more like," Jane scoffed.

"Let him finish, love," Harold said.

"I just want to talk to Erica," Smith pleaded. "If she tells me to leave, I'll leave, but I have to try."

"She doesn't want to talk to you," Jane wasn't yielding. "So *I'm* telling you to leave."

"Jane," Harold had raised his voice. "Let's let Erica decide. I'll see if she's up to it."

He left the room before his wife could argue.

He returned a short while later.

"She's in the living room," he told Smith.

"Thank you," Smith tried to smile at him but he was on the verge of tears and the smile wouldn't come.

He walked past Jane into the hallway. Whitton's mother was shaking her head.

Whitton was sitting in an armchair when Smith came in. Her face was red, and her eyes were puffy. She looked like she'd been crying.

"Erica," Smith said gently and crouched down in front of her chair. "I'm so sorry."

Whitton didn't speak. She didn't even look at him.

"I'm sorry," Smith said again. "I don't know what else to say. I made a huge mistake and I'm sorry."

Their eyes met and in that moment Smith realised two things. If Whitton took him back, he would never let anything like what happened with Baldwin happen ever again, and if she refused to take him back he would do everything he could to make her change her mind. No matter what it took, he never wanted to see that look in Whitton's eyes again. Her once, mischievous, sparkling green eyes were now lifeless. It was as though what Smith had done to her had drained her of all her spirit.

She broke eye contact and her head dipped.

"You don't have to say anything," Smith told her. "But please listen to what I have to say. I know I've hurt you deeply. I know that. I can't take back what I did, but I can promise you something. I will do anything to have you back in my life. Whatever it takes, just tell me what to do. I know it will take time, but I'll wait as long as you need me to."

Whitton raised her head and looked at him again. Her mouth opened. "Why?"

It was all she said and Smith didn't know how to reply. He really couldn't understand how it had happened.

"I don't know," he said and realised it wasn't the answer Whitton needed to hear. "It happened and I don't know why. I've never done anything like that before, and I don't understand it. But I want to make things right. I want you and Laura back."

Whitton's face hardened at the mention of their daughter. "Don't you dare bring Laura into this. Don't you dare."

"Erica," Smith said.

"I can't even look at you right now," she said. "You disgust me. You make me sick."

"I'm sorry."

"Oh, I know you're sorry – you're sorry for yourself. Poor Jason, all alone. You're pathetic."

"I love you, Erica," Smith said. "I love you more than anything else on earth."

"Get out," Whitton's face was now filled with fury. "Get out and never come back here."

Smith knew he had outstayed his welcome. He got to his feet and left the room without saying anything further.

He popped his head in the kitchen. "Thank you for letting me see her."

"I'll see you out," Harold said.

Whitton's mother didn't say a word.

"It didn't go too well," Smith told Harold on the doorstep.

"What did you expect, son?"

"Pretty much what happened," Smith admitted.

"She needs time. She needs all the time you can give her. At least she's letting off a bit of steam now. I couldn't help overhear her in there. That's good. Up until now all she's done is sit and stare into space."

"Thank you, Harold," Smith said.

Harold placed his hand on Smith's shoulder. "One step at a time, son."

He left his hand on the shoulder and Smith sensed he wanted to say something else.

"One step at a time," Smith was right. "But if you ever hurt my baby girl again, I'll make sure you're eating through a straw for the rest of your life."

CHAPTER FORTY

"This isn't the news I wanted to wake up to this morning," DCI Chalmers barked. "From what I can gather the murder of Father Jacob Swift puts us one step back. Does anyone have anything that will put me in a better mood this morning?"

Once more the team was gathered for a briefing. Bridge, Yang Chu, Baldwin and Grant Webber sat with blank expressions on their faces. Webber's technician, Harry was nowhere to be seen.

"Anyone?" Chalmers said.

"Where's your assistant?" Yang Chu asked Webber.

"I let him have the morning off," Webber said. "After his early morning wake-up I thought I'd give him a few hours to catch up on some sleep."

Yang Chu had decided to wait a while before telling Webber about the way Harry had behaved at the crime scene. Perhaps there was a perfectly innocent explanation for his actions after all.

"I suppose we start from the beginning again," Chalmers sighed. "Unless anyone has any other suggestions."

"We need Smith," Bridge said out of the blue.

"I agree," Yang Chu seconded.

Baldwin remained silent.

"Smith is taking some time off," Chalmers reminded them.

"He doesn't want time off," Yang Chu said. "I've spoken to him and the last thing he needs right now is time off. This investigation has hit a standstill and we need Smith to come up with something new."

Chalmers appeared to be mulling this over. He rubbed his eyes.

"I suppose you're right. Smyth is away for the next couple of days anyway so there's no danger of them bumping into each other. I'll get hold of Smith.

In the meantime, do we know anything about the murder of Father Swift yet? Any witnesses? Have we spoken with next of kin?"

"Apparently he didn't have any," Yang Chu opened his notebook. "No wife or kids and no brothers or sisters."

"Married to the church then," Chalmers said. "What about the initial forensics?"

"The knife in his back was what killed him," Webber said. "It was a Kila dagger, similar to the ones found at the previous three murders. No message on his phone, but Harry found a note in his pocket."

"I copied it," Yang Chu said and read from his notebook. *The path of the righteous man is beset on all sides by the inequities of the selfish and the tyranny of evil men.*

These are the demons of humanity, and I have taken them from you. I Googled it and the first part is from the Old Testament. Ezekiel 25, but I couldn't find any reference to the bit about demons anywhere."

"It's along the same vein as the messages on the phones," Bridge said. "About taking demons. This man is a real nutcase."

"So," Chalmers said. "We can assume this is the work of the same killer then, but where does it lead us? Usually in a murder investigation the more bodies that turn up, the more information we have, but this appears to be the opposite. Just when we were about to bring the good Father Swift in for questioning someone takes it upon themselves to knock him off. What the hell is happening here? Why kill a man of the church?"

"What if the killer knew we were going to interview him?" Yang Chu said. "And killed him to prevent him from speaking to us?"

"If that's the case then we have to assume Father Swift did know something. What did he know that made someone murder him?"

"We need to have a closer look at the church," Bridge said.

"I agree," Chalmers said. "Webber, I want you and your team to go over St Olave's with a fine-toothed comb."

"What are we supposed to be looking for?" Webber asked.

"I don't know. Something that shouldn't be there."

"I'll get onto it."

"Sir," Yang Chu couldn't keep quiet any longer. "What do you know about Webber's new technician?"

"Harry?" Chalmers said. "Not much. I believe he actually requested a transfer to work alongside the great Grant Webber. Word is he took a dip in his wages."

"Where did he work before?"

"I have no idea. What's this got to do with the investigation?"

"I think there's something odd about him, that's all."

"Then he'll fit in well around here won't he? If there's nothing else for the time being, I'll let you grab some coffee. I'm going to let Smith know how much you miss him, and we'll reconvene in an hour."

* * *

Smith was deciding whether to fetch a beer from the fridge when Chalmers phoned. It was only ten in the morning, but Smith didn't have anything else to do. When he saw Chalmers' name on the screen he debated whether to reject the call but he couldn't do it.

"What's up, boss?"

"Your unofficial suspension has been lifted," Chalmers got straight to the point. "Get your arse in here now."

"What brought about the change of heart?" Smith asked.

"I'm in a charitable mood."

"What about Smyth?"

"Superintendent Smyth is away for a few days, so I decided out of the kindness of my heart to let you come back to work."

"You've hit a brick wall haven't you?" Smith said.

"Cheeky bastard. Just make sure you're here within the next half hour."

"I'll think about it," Smith said. "I'll give it some serious thought."

With that he rang off.

CHAPTER FORTY ONE

"He's leaving the house now," the man told the woman on the other end of the line. "He's getting into his car."

"Follow him," she said. "See where he goes."

"I thought the plan was to surprise him at home."

"It still is, but I want to see what he's poking his nose into now. We need to keep a keen eye on him."

"He's pulling away from the kerb," the man said.

"Keep him in your sights, but don't let him figure out you're following him."

"I'm not a bloody hit man. What do I know about tailing someone?"

"Just don't lose him," the woman said. "And, Hal?'

"What?"

"You are a hit man – that's exactly what you are. You are a hit man for a higher power than anyone could possibly imagine."

* * *

Smith pulled away from the kerb and turned right at the end of the street. He followed the road across the river and took a left to bypass the busy city centre. He glanced in the rearview mirror and then looked again. There was a black hatchback behind him he was sure had been parked down the road from his house earlier. He carried on for a couple of hundred metres and checked again. The black car was still there, now two cars behind him. Smith turned left at the next traffic lights then turned left again. Another left and he was back on the same road he'd been on a few minutes earlier. The black car was now nowhere to be seen.

I'm being paranoid, he thought. *What's making me so paranoid?*

He was a few hundred metres away from the police station when he spotted it. The black car was back. Smith reached the station and turned into the car park. The black car carried on along the road and disappeared in the distance. Smith couldn't be certain of what had just happened. There were plenty of black cars and what Smith knew about car models was next to nothing. He pushed his paranoia aside and went inside the station.

PC Hugo Limpet was manning the front desk and Smith was glad he wouldn't have to bump into Baldwin straight away. Then he remembered that Baldwin had been brought in to help with the murder investigation. He nodded to Limpet. "Morning."

"Is it still morning?' the unfortunately-named PC said. "It doesn't feel like it. I've been here for almost ten hours."

"Lucky you," Smith said and headed for the canteen.

Bridge and Yang Chu were the sole occupants of the canteen. Smith chose his usual coffee from the machine and joined them.

"That was quick," Bridge said. "Were you waiting in your car in the car park waiting for Chalmers to beg you back?"

"You've hit a brick wall haven't you?" Smith asked him the same thing he'd asked Chalmers. "You need me don't you?"

"We're running short of ideas," Bridge admitted. "And you have an unusually warped mind. I reckon that's why you've managed to catch so many unusually warped-minded killers."

"I'll take that as a compliment. Chalmers' request sounded rather urgent and yet here you are sitting drinking coffee like the killer of four dead men can wait."

"The DCI gave us a break until you got here," Yang Chu explained. "He's called another briefing in fifteen minutes."

"Ha," Smith said. "I told you you needed me."

Twenty-five-minutes later they sat once more in the room where not much had been achieved in the past week. Four men were dead and all they were sure of was the same person was responsible for the murders. That was it. They had no idea of a motive, very little evidence to point towards anyone in particular and they were no closer now than they were after Peter Ashe's body was discovered with his manhood removed.

"Smith," Chalmers said. "I'll let you take over once more. It's been fun – just like old times but I think a fresh head is what we need right now." Smith spent the next forty-five-minutes going over the series events from when Peter Ashe's wife found his body right up to the discovery in St Olave's Church early that morning. The team let him talk. When he was finished he looked around the room at the tired faces, and frowned.

"What jumps out at you? Is there any particular aspect of this whole investigation that just jumps out? Something that strikes you as odd?"

"I still can't figure out how the killer knew about the confessions," Bridge was the first one to talk. "I've gone over and over it in my head and there is no way the killer could find out about what these men confessed to and then kill them in such a short space of time."

"I agree," Yang Chu said. "Peter Ashe was killed a few hours after he spoke to Father Swift as was John Ware. We don't have the final path report on Alex Power but I bet we'll find the same thing with him. It's as though the killer was in the confessional booth *with* these men."

"We've overlooked the fact that Father Swift could have contacted the killer shortly after the confessions," Baldwin chipped in. "He could have phoned them."

"I don't buy that," Smith said. "Father Swift was very guarded over the sanctity of the confession. There is no way he would break that confidence."

"What then?" Yang Chu said. "How was the murderer able to act so quickly?"

"I don't know," Smith admitted. "I really don't know. Let's not waste time speculating about what we don't know and go over what we do. All four men were killed with an unusual knife. A Tibetan Kila dagger. We know one of its uses is to remove demons and that fact is reiterated in the messages the dead men received. We don't know where these knives came from, and as

Baldwin pointed out it would take months to go through the numerous channels one can use to obtain such a knife. What else do we know?"

"What happened to the missing body parts?" Yang Chu asked.

"Good question," Smith said. "A penis, a pair of hands and a couple of eyes are missing in action. Why did the killer take them away with him? What purpose would that serve?"

"Maybe he believed the demons were in the body parts," Yang Chu suggested. "That's why they had to be taken away from the bodies."

"I reckon the killer still has them," Bridge said. "They could be some form of trophy."

"In that case we've got a clash of motives," Smith pointed out. "If what we know about the Kila knife is true and the demons are drawn out of the body and trapped in the knives, why take the body parts away if they are in fact where the demons are hidden? It doesn't make any sense."

"Nothing in this investigation has made any sense," Baldwin said.

"OK," Smith decided on a change of tack. "We have four dead men but one of them doesn't fit."

"Father Swift," Yang Chu said.

"Exactly. Father Swift was killed with a Kila knife but that's as far as the similarity to the others goes. He was stabbed in the back, but he didn't have any of his body parts removed, nor did he receive a message on his mobile phone after he was killed."

"There was a message in his pocket," Yang Chu reminded him.

"But that message was completely different to the others," Smith said. "The only similarity was that it also mentioned something about demons."

"The demons of humanity," Yang Chu elaborated. "Not the demons inside Father Swift himself."

"No," Smith said. "And one way to interpret that is the killer has taken it upon himself to assume Father Swift's role as a cleanser of souls, but his method is much more extreme. Instead of hearing confessions and offering absolution, he listens to confessions and absolves the sinners by killing them and containing their demons inside the daggers."

The room was silent. It was so quiet that when Chalmers' mobile phone started to ring on the table in front of him, everybody jumped.

Chalmers picked it up and answered it. "Webber, what have you got?"

The team watched as Chalmers listened to what the Head of Forensics had to tell him. The conversation was one-sided. It was clear Webber was finished when the DCI spoke.

"Are you one hundred percent certain of this?"

The expression on Chalmers' face told the team that Webber had answered in the affirmative. His eyes grew wide, and then closed.

"Well," Chalmers said when he'd ended the call. "That's one mystery out of the way. Webber found something in St Olave's Church that definitely shouldn't be there."

"Boss?" Smith urged.

"A hidden microphone," Chalmers said. "There was a hidden microphone inside the confessional booth. That's how the bastard knew what these men had confessed to."

CHAPTER FORTY TWO

"Why didn't we think of that?" Smith said. "It was so obvious."

"Everything's obvious when you know the answers, Sarge," Yang Chu said.

"Very deep," Bridge scoffed. "What is that? Some pillar of wisdom from Vietnamese religion?"

"It's called stating the obvious," Yang Chu retorted. "It's true. And who would ever think of looking for a hidden microphone in a confessional booth? The whole idea is preposterous."

"At least we know how the killer knew what these men had done," Smith said.

"Is there any way to trace the signal?" Baldwin asked. "Trace it back to whoever is listening in?"

"I think it's too late for that," Yang Chu replied. "We could probably trace it if the receiver was getting the signal from the mic but now we've found the microphone the killer will know we're onto them and will switch off the receiver."

"No," Smith shouted. "No, no, no."

"What are you thinking?" Chalmers asked him. "I know that look."

"Where is the microphone now?"

"I assume Webber has taken it back with him."

"He needs to put it back."

"What are you talking about?" Chalmers said.

"Webber needs to put that mic back before the murderer realises it's been found. We can use it to set a trap."

"A fake confession, you mean?" Bridge had cottoned on.

"Exactly. We can use it to lure the killer into a trap."

"Sarge," it was Yang Chu. "Aren't you forgetting something? Father Swift is dead – who's going to hear the confession?"

"Father Swift isn't the only churchman in York," Smith said. "St Olave's isn't about to crumble to the ground because he's no longer with us. I've got a good feeling that this could work."

"It's worth a try," Chalmers agreed. "I'll let Webber know the plan and get the ball rolling."

While Chalmers was putting Smith's plan into action Smith had decided it would be a good idea to speak to the relatives of the dead men again in light of this new information. Bridge had gone to speak with John Ware's mother again and Baldwin had offered to see if Alex Power's wife could tell them anything. She had returned from her business trip to Wales.

Smith parked his car outside Penelope Slyper's house. He assumed Peter Ashe's wife, Heidi would still be there. Smith and Yang Chu walked up the path and Smith knocked on the door. If Penelope Slyper's face had shown her displeasure at seeing Smith and Yang Chu the last time they met this expression could only be described as a face of thunder. She looked absolutely furious.

"Unless you've come to inform my sister that you've caught the bastard who killed her husband you can leave right now."

"We need to speak to Mrs Ashe again," Smith said.

"She's said all she's going to say."

Smith was getting tired of this. "Miss Slyper, we can have a quiet chat here or we can deposit Mrs Ashe in a car and drive her to the police station and do it there. Which do you reckon she would prefer?"

"You can't do this. You cannot keep harassing my sister."

"I'm afraid we can," Smith informed her. "We can keep it up until this case is closed. Now could you please let us in? The neighbours are getting curious." This was a lie, but it seemed to have the desired result. Penelope Slyper stepped outside to look for any evidence of curtain twitching.

Heidi Ashe was sitting in the same chair in the living room where she'd been the last time Smith spoke to her. He wondered if she'd actually moved since then.

"Mrs Ashe, sorry to arrive unannounced, but we need to ask you a few more questions."

"I tried to get rid of them," Penelope told her. "But they got all heavy-handed."

"That will be all, Miss Slyper," Smith said, more to annoy her than anything else.

This studded woman was really starting to rub him up the wrong way.

"We'll call you if we need anything," he added.

Smith and Yang Chu sat on a large leather sofa.

"Mrs Ashe," Smith began. "Did you know Father Jacob Swift?"

"Peter used to speak of him, but I never met him. I'm afraid I'm not too big on religion. It sounds terrible but I just don't believe."

"It's not terrible. When we were last here you mentioned something about Peter not being religious when you met."

"Did I?"

"Yes. And you said he suddenly became religious. Do you remember what made him change his mind?"

"I told you I don't know why he suddenly found a taste for the church. Maybe it was after his first affair. Maybe he developed a conscience and thought that going to church would absolve him of his sins. How on earth would I know?"

Because he was your husband, Smith thought but held his tongue.

"Did you know Peter went to Father Swift to confess?" Yang Chu asked.

"It would make sense. That's all the confession is really isn't it? You sin, you confess, you're absolved and so on and so on. It doesn't really change anything does it?"

"What do you mean?" Smith asked her.

"Well, the confession eases the conscience, but it doesn't stop you repeating what you confessed about does it? In that way I find the church to be merely a society of hypocrites. Who are they to assume the power of absolution? Who gave them that power? There are greater forces out there than the likes of Father Swift, I can tell you that."

"What do you mean?" Smith was intrigued.

"It would take all day to explain and you probably wouldn't understand anyway. If you'll excuse me, I need to use the bathroom."

Yang Chu frowned at Smith and twirled his index finger next to his temple to imply Heidi Ashe was a couple of cards short of a full deck. Smith looked around the room and his gaze rested on the photograph on the mantelpiece again. He stood up and picked up the photograph. The scenery really was breath-taking. The monastery in the foreground was lit up by the sun. The photographer had obviously taken the shot with the sun behind him. The sheer cliffs with the clear blue sky behind formed a perfect background. Penelope Slyper was smiling in the photograph, and the absence of piercings gave her face a softer appearance. Smith's eyes fell on the man. The ridiculous goatee beard aside, he wasn't a bad-looking man. His expression was more serious as though reflecting the sombre nature of the location. Smith stared at him hard – he was certain he'd seen him before, but he still couldn't work out who he was.

"This bloke's face is bugging me," he said to Yang Chu. "He looks familiar but I still can't place him."

Yang Chu stood up to get a closer look.

"Is that Metal Mickey?" he pointed to the woman.

Smith laughed. "She does look a lot better without all those piercings.

"You know who that looks like," Yang Chu placed his finger on the man's face.

"I told you, I can't place him."

"It is," Yang Chu said. "It is him. He's a bit younger there, but I'm ninety-nine percent certain that's Harry, Webber's new technician."

CHAPTER FORTY THREE

"Are you absolutely sure it's him?" Smith asked Yang Chu as they drove away from Penelope Slyper's house.

They had excused themselves and told Heidi Ashe that they had no more questions. Penelope had glared at them as they left.

"Positive," Yang Chu said. "He looks a bit older now but that was definitely him. Those eyes and the shape of his nose are unmistakable. What does it mean?"

"I don't know," Smith said. "I honestly don't know. It could be nothing – one of those four degrees of separation things. You know where the world's getting smaller and you'll find someone you know knows someone who knows someone you know. If you get my drift. But this is quite a coincidence don't you think?"

"And you hate coincidence."

"Exactly. What are the odds on the sister-in-law of the first victim being in a photograph with one of our forensics technicians?"

"Very high," Yang Chu said. "And his odd behaviour recently makes it even more suspicious. I think we need to do some background checking on this Harry bloke."

"That might be a problem," Smith said. "How do you suggest we do that? Approach Webber and tell him his latest protégé seems a bit iffy to us and we'd like to know some more about him?"

"And Webber seems to think the sun shines out of this bloke's arse," Yang Chu added.

"Then we won't involve Webber. If it turns out it is a coincidence Harry bumped into Penelope Slyper on a gap-year trip around the Himalayas then Webber never needs to know. But if there is something going on, he'll understand why we couldn't involve him."

"The bloke's dodgy," Yang Chu said. "I can feel it."

"I'm starving," Smith announced when they were halfway back to the station. "I can't actually remember the last time I ate anything. I haven't had much of an appetite. Let's do something normal working-class people do – let's take a lunch hour."

He received no arguments from Yang Chu and they settled on a new Chinese restaurant a stone's throw away from the station.

"I'm buying," Smith added. "As a way of thanking you for all your Agony Aunt advice."

"Why are all Chinese restaurants lacking in the originality department?" Yang Chu asked as they went inside the New Wok Inn, on Finch Street. "They're all the same. I reckon if someone opened up a Chinese place and named it the Peking Grouse, they'd make a killing from the curiosity factor alone."

"You have a very special imagination," Smith said. "And I don't mean *special* in a good way."

They chose a table by the window. They had a Wednesday lunchtime special running.

"That's why you offered to pay," Yang Chu said. "You knew about the Wednesday special."

"I've never been here before," Smith insisted.

The waiter arrived and handed them a couple of menus. Smith felt like a beer, but he ordered two cokes instead. He opted for a Beef Chow Mein and Yang Chu ordered the vegetarian version.

"That photograph is bugging me," Smith said while they waited for the food. "Something about the way they were standing suggested it was more than just two people who had met at a Tibetan monastery. They were too close – intimate even."

"Maybe we should have just asked Mrs Ashe's sister," Yang Chu said.

"She's hardly been forthcoming with information so far. She probably would have told us to mind our own business, and to be honest, we don't have any proof to suggest that it's even relevant to the investigation."

"Have you spoken to Whitton yet?" Yang Chu asked and Smith was glad when the waiter arrived with their food.

It was a question he didn't feel like answering and the reception he'd received at Whitton's parents' house that morning wasn't something he felt like relating to anyone.

"That's better," Smith pushed the empty plate away from him. Yang Chu still had half of his left. "You really were hungry. These beans are tough. I reckon we'd have got much better food at the Peking Grouse."

Smith laughed, and his mobile phone started to ring inside his pocket.

"Too slow," he said and took it out. "I've finished eating. Beat you."

He looked at the screen.

"Boss," he said to DCI Chalmers.

"Where are you?"

"Just around the corner." It was the truth.

"Is Yang Chu still with you?"

"Yes," Smith sensed that something had happened. "What's wrong?"

"My office as soon as you get back."

"What did Chalmers want?" Yang Chu said and placed his knife and fork on the plate.

The beans had beaten him.

"He didn't say," Smith said. "He just told us to get back to the station, but I know that tone of voice. Something has happened."

"Hopefully it's good news. Maybe Webber has had a bite on the hidden microphone."

"Maybe," Smith said. "Even though he had a feeling what Chalmers was going to tell them wasn't good news at all."

CHAPTER FORTY FOUR

Smith's gut instinct was rarely wrong and when he saw the expression on Chalmers' face he knew straight away it hadn't been this time either.

"Sit down," the DCI told Smith and Yang Chu.

"What's going on, boss?" Smith asked. "Am I suspended again?"

"Shut up. There's been an allegation made. A serious allegation."

Smith tried to think of what he might have done recently to warrant a serious allegation being brought up against him but nothing jumped out at him."

"What have I done?"

"You haven't done anything," Chalmers replied. "For once this is not about you."

His gaze fell on Yang Chu.

"Me?" the young DC looked stunned. "What did I do?"

"Contaminating a crime scene," Chalmers said. "Interfering with evidence. Do I need to go on?"

"With respect, sir, I have no idea what you're talking about."

"You were called out to the scene of Father Swift's murder?"

"That's right."

"And do I need to remind you of the procedure when entering a potential crime scene?"

"Sir?"

"Did you put on the required Scene of Crime Suit?"

"No, but."

"I see. You ought to know better, DC Yang Chu. If this was an official complaint, I would be obliged to make a report and it would go on your record. Luckily for you all I'm obliged to do is hand out a severe bollocking."

"Who made the complaint?" Yang Chu was still in shock.

"That's not important."

"Of course it's important," Smith joined in. "Who made the allegation, boss? Don't tell me, it was Super Harry, Webber's new boy. Because if it was, the bloke's not so squeaky clean himself."

"What are you going on about?" Chalmers said.

"Tell him," Smith said to Yang Chu.

"Firstly, sir," Yang Chu said. "I didn't go anywhere near Father Swift. I stopped right inside the door of the church. Webber's tech made it absolutely clear he wished to work in peace. I thought this was highly unorthodox, so I hid behind one of the pews and watched him."

"You spied on forensics?"

"Hear him out, boss."

"Harry wasn't wearing a SOC suit," Yang Chu continued. "He wasn't even wearing gloves, sir, and I watched as he pulled the Kila knife out of Father Swift's back with his bare hands. He is the one who contaminated the crime scene and interfered with evidence, not me. It was dimly lit in there so I couldn't see exactly what was happening, but it looked like he bent over and searched Father Swift's pocket."

"Could've been looking for ID," Chalmers suggested.

"Or he could have been putting something *inside* the pocket, and not taking something out."

"The note, boss," Smith elaborated.

"I'm not an idiot, Smith, I knew what Yang Chu was insinuating. And believe you me that's all it is – an insinuation. Did anybody else see what this Harry bloke was up to?"

"I told you, sir, he made sure that uniform were out of view."

"Then it's his word against yours. There's nothing we can do."

Smith told Chalmers about the photograph of Harry in Penelope Slyper's house.

"Don't you think that's a bit of a coincidence? That Webber's new technician just happens to know the sister of the first victim?"

"Coincidences do happen," Chalmers said. "Even though you don't think so. I told you, there's nothing we can do. Now, I have a lot of work to catch up on – I'm sure with you back at the helm you can do without me at the case meeting."

"Boss," Smith said. "There's something going on here with that Harry bloke."

"Leave it, Smith. We've got enough to worry about with these four murders. You're bloody lucky old Smyth is away – you'd be heading up another press conference by now. Forget about Harry the technician and come up with something that will help crack this investigation. It's starting to give me a headache."

As Smith walked away from Chalmers' office, he was becoming more and more convinced that Webber's new assistant was not what he appeared to be. He didn't feel like digging around at the New Forensics Building – the place always gave him the creeps.

"I have to go out for a bit," he told Yang Chu.

"Where are you going?"

"It's better you don't know."

"Chalmers didn't even apologise for getting the wrong end of the stick about me allegedly contaminating a crime scene," Yang Chu said.

"You know that's never going to happen."

* * *

Smith stopped once more outside Penelope Slyper's house. He'd been there so many times in the past few days that it felt like his car had driven there on autopilot. It was like déjà vu – Smith waiting outside the door and Penelope Slyper opening it with an even darker look in her eyes. Even her piercings seemed more menacing this time.

"This is getting beyond a joke," she said although she was clearly not finding it amusing. "Do I need to file a harassment charge?"

"There's no need to be like that. This will be the last time I come here, I promise."

Smith didn't know it then but he would break that promise before the day was over.

"Heidi isn't here, so you're wasting your time. Goodbye."

"It's actually you I came to speak to," Smith told her.

"What about? And why can't you police just say everything you need to say in one go? Why do you have to keep coming back?"

"Have you ever watched Colombo, Miss Slyper?"

"Of course."

"Good. You know that quirk of his where you think he's finished and then he turns around and says, *just one more thing*?"

"What are you talking about?"

"I'm a bit like Colombo," Smith said. "Only it takes me a bit longer to think of that *one more thing*. My brain obviously works a lot slower than his. Can I please come inside?"

"Make it quick. I'm expecting an important phone call shortly and I expect you to be gone by the time I take it."

Smith found himself in the living room. He made a beeline for the photograph on the mantelpiece but it was no longer there.

"Well," Penelope said. "What is it you wanted to ask me?"

"There was a photograph here earlier," Smith pointed to where it had been. "Where is it?"

"Oh that. Heidi slammed the sideboard door again and it fell off. It keeps happening so she moved it."

"Where is it?"

"What's so important about an old photograph?"

"Where is it?" Smith asked again.

"I imagine she put it somewhere else. You'll have to ask her next time you feel like popping in uninvited."

She said this with such cattiness, Smith had the urge to arrest her for obstruction of justice. The charge wouldn't stick of course, but it would cause her some inconvenience.

He put his hand on the handle of the sideboard. "Maybe she put it in here."

Penelope yanked his hand away. "It's not in there. I tidied up the sideboard just before you arrived and it's not in there."

Smith looked at her. Her eyes told him she was afraid of him finding something. He'd seen that look before. He put some distance between him and the sideboard.

"OK," he said. "Just one more thing, who is the man in the photograph?"

"Just some bloke I met."

"Do you remember his name?"

"Hal," she said. "He called himself Hal."

CHAPTER FORTY FIVE

Smith parked his car round the corner from Penelope Slyper's house and took out his phone. He dialled Chalmers' number.

"What now?" the DCI's mood obviously hadn't improved.

"Boss," Smith said. "I need some backup at this address."

He gave Chalmers Penelope's address.

"And I need a search warrant.'

"What the hell for?"

"I have a strong feeling that we're going to find something in that house – something linked to the recent murders."

"What makes you think that?"

"Penelope Slyper, she's the first victim's sister-in-law. I'm convinced she's hiding something."

"You know I can't just pluck a warrant out of thin air. It takes time."

"Then just organise back-up. Now. I'll play the delay card on the search warrant. I'll take the flak for any fallout."

"What?"

"If a police officer believes there is every chance that vital evidence could be destroyed or removed due to the delay in obtaining a warrant," Smith quoted directly from the law he'd learned. "And therefore the ends of justice would be defeated, I can use my discretion. Get me some help here. It doesn't matter who it is – I just need someone to corroborate my story. It can be a fucking traffic warden for all I care."

He ended the call knowing full well that Chalmers would be spitting bullets right now, but he would still do what Smith had just asked.

Smith was proved right just ten minutes later, and he was more than relieved when he discovered that Chalmers hadn't sent a traffic warden to his rescue. Yang Chu's Ford Focus parked behind him, and the young DC and Bridge got out.

"Where's the fire?" Yang Chu said.

"Around the corner at Penelope Slyper's house," Smith replied. "Am I glad Chalmers sent you two."

"Do you think we're in for a bit of action?" Bridge asked.

"Let's go and find out."

Smith didn't even knock this time. He opened the door and went straight inside. Bridge and Yang Chu followed him. Penelope Slyper was on the phone in the kitchen. She stopped, mid-sentence and stared at the three detectives who had barged into her house.

"What the hell..."

"End the call," Smith said and grabbed the phone out of her hand. "Let's go and see if that photograph is in the sideboard shall we? You can come with us and bear witness that we're not doing anything untoward."

He stormed down the corridor and into the living room. He opened the sideboard. The photograph wasn't there. There were three large drawers contained inside the sideboard with a shelf that ran on top of all three. The shelf appeared to contain various correspondence and nothing much else. Letters, most of them bills were stacked neatly on top of each other. Smith opened the first drawer. Inside was a small glass jar that had been painted black. The paint meant it was impossible to see what was inside. Smith took out a pair of gloves, put them on and picked it up. The lid was fastened tightly but Smith could feel there was some kind of liquid inside."

"What's this?" he asked Penelope.

"I don't know," she replied. "I've never seen it before."

If I had a pound for every time I've heard that, Smith thought. *I wouldn't be here now. I definitely wouldn't be here now.*

He opened the second drawer and an unpleasant smell hit his nostrils. A thick brown cloth was covering something bulky. Smith carefully removed the cloth to reveal a large white plastic envelope with a zip. Smith slowly opened the zip and discovered the source of the stench. Inside were two pale hands. The skin had turned bluish black in places and the area where they had been severed from the arm was now completely black.

"Jesus Christ," Bridge had caught a glimpse of them.

The third drawer was opened and Smith looked inside. Two bulging eyeballs stared back at him, unseeing. He turned to look at Penelope Slyper. Her face was extremely pale and clammy and she looked like she might pass out any moment.

"Get everyone here," Smith told Yang Chu. "I want this place turned upside down. "Bridge, do you want to take Miss Slyper here through to the kitchen and give her a glass of water – she's not looking too hot. You can inform her that she's under arrest at the same time. Good God. What a mess."

Smith had walked past Yang Chu and was almost out of the house when he turned around.

"Yang Chu," he called.

Yang Chu popped his head round the door. "Sarge?"

"When Webber gets here, tell him I left whatever is in that black jar alone. He can have the pleasure of opening it. We wouldn't want to be accused of contaminating a crime scene would we?"

"I'll make sure of it, Sarge."

CHAPTER FORTY SIX

Smith waited for the reinforcements to arrive then drove away without a word of explanation to anyone. The events of the past week had finally caught up with him. It wasn't so much the investigation – although he had to admit this was one of the most draining he'd ever worked on, it was what was happening between him and Whitton that was taking more of a toll. What he felt like now could only be described as feeling as if there was a gaping hole inside him. It was a hole that seemed to be getting bigger and bigger and he felt powerless to stop it. His mobile phone started to ring before he'd even parked the car outside his house. Whitton's car was still being fixed so there was space on the driveway but somehow it didn't feel right parking there. He wondered if he would end up parking there even if she never came back home.

When he got inside his house, he'd already forgotten his phone had rang. The house was far too quiet. Smith felt a deep longing for some kind of familiarity and when he opened the back door and the dogs jumped up at him he got it for a short while. He fed Theakston and Fred – he fed them much more than he usually did and when he saw they'd both left food in their bowls he started to cry. It wasn't the fact that the overweight Bull Terrier and the ugly Pug had left some food, it was just the last straw in a week that had been the worst of his life.

Smith was still sobbing when he opened the fridge and took out a beer. He wiped his eyes on his sleeve and went outside for a smoke. His next-door-neighbour was trimming his hedge when Smith got outside. Smith lit a cigarette and ignored him. He was halfway through the beer when he heard the last words he really wanted to hear right now.

"Can I have a word?"

You're going to tell me anyway, Smith thought. *Whether I want to hear it or not.*

He took another swig of beer and looked at his neighbour. He really didn't know what it was about the man – was it the fact that he never stopped moaning about trivial things, or because he was just naturally irritating, but he'd never been able to warm to the man.

"Are you alright?" his neighbour asked.

"What?"

Smith was in a state of shock.

"I'm fine. Rough week."

"What was it?" the man wasn't quite finished. "Neglect of household duties or playing away from home. It was usually the latter in my case."

"Excuse me?" Smith had no idea what he was talking about.

"My Glenda," Smith was clearly about to be enlightened. "Left me sixteen times in the first ten years."

"Sixteen times?" Smith finished what was left in the bottle.

"That was the first ten years, mind. They reckon they're the hardest. You're still adjusting then, you see. She started hitting the road less often after that."

Smith felt something happen inside. He was actually amused. This petty little man from next door was actually cheering him up.

"But she always came back?"

"She's still inside, knitting God-knows what for God-knows who."

"How long have you been married?" Smith asked him.

"Too long, but not long enough. They drive you to drink, as you probably already know, but when they're not around the drink doesn't taste so good anymore. You'll be alright. First time's the worst. I'd better get back. I only came outside because that incessant click-clacking was starting to really piss me off."

"Thank you," Smith said. "Thank you."

"For what?"

"I have no idea."

When Smith went back inside he wasn't sure what had just happened. He'd lived next to his neighbour for more years than he could remember – he didn't even know the man's name, and he realised he'd just said more to the man in five minutes than he had in all those years.

And the man wasn't as bad as he thought.

He's just a normal bloke, he thought. *A normal bloke with normal problems.* He got another beer from the fridge and took it through to the living room. Theakston and Fred were already snoring on the sofa. Smith had fed them far too much food. He knew if Whitton had seen how much food he'd put in their bowls, she'd be disgusted. His phone started to ring again and he ignored it again.

He sat down next to the dogs and picked up his phone. He brought up Whitton's number and pressed, *call*. It rang three times and he cancelled the call. He didn't know what he was going to say and he didn't feel like being screamed at. He decided to send her a message instead. He opened up his messages and began.

Erica, I'm sorry. I'm sorry and if I could go back and change one part of my life that part would be it. I need you. I need you and Laura. I overfed the dogs.

He stopped writing there when a new message arrived. It was from Yang Chu.

Sarge, it read. *Phone me. We've interviewed Penelope Slyper and the man in the photograph is definitely Hal Grimes. Harry Grimes. It's Webber's bloke. And the woman isn't Penelope – it's her sister, Heidi. Phone me urgently.*

CHAPTER FORTY SEVEN

Thirty minutes earlier

"Interview with Penelope Slyper commenced, 16:38," Chalmers said. "Present Miss Slyper, DCI Chalmers and DC Yang Chu. Miss Slyper, do you understand why you were arrested?"

"You've made a mistake," Penelope said. "A huge mistake. She's gone. Heidi and Hal have gone."

"Hal?" Chalmers said. "Who is Hal?"

"Harry Grimes. Heidi thinks he's some kind of God."

"Miss Slyper," Chalmers said. "Some unusual items were found in the sideboard in your house. Can you explain how they got there?"

"I didn't even know they were there until that detective opened up the drawers."

"For the record," Chalmers said. "What Miss Slyper is referring to is the following: A penis in a jar of embalming fluid, two hands and a pair of eyeballs. Miss Slyper, what were they doing in your house?"

"I don't know. I told you I didn't know they were there."

"Didn't you notice the smell?" Yang Chu asked. "The smell was quite obvious when we opened up the sideboard."

"I very rarely have cause to go in the sideboard," Penelope said. "I didn't put them there."

"Who did, then?" Chalmers said.

Penelope bowed her head and rubbed her eyes.

"No comment," she said to the table.

"Miss Slyper," Chalmers said. "Do you understand how serious this is? Three men have been murdered. One had his penis removed, another had both hands severed and the third had his eyeballs gouged out. We found all of these body parts inside your house. It really isn't looking good for you."

"I don't know anything about it," Penelope said.

"OK," Chalmers said. "We know you killed those men – the evidence is pretty much cut and dry, but what I want to know is why you did it? Why did you kill these men and why cut off parts of their body?"

"I can't stand the sight of blood," Penelope said. "There is no way I could kill anyone, let alone cut off pieces of them."

"Father Jacob Swift," Chalmers said. "Why did you kill him? What did he know that was so damning you had to kill him for it?"

Penelope started to cry. "I didn't kill Father Swift. He was my friend. I don't know why they had to…"

She stopped there.

"Miss Slyper?" Chalmers urged. "You were going to say something."

"No comment," Penelope sobbed.

"They?" Chalmers said. "By they do you mean Heidi and this Hal man?"

"No comment."

"Penelope," Yang Chu said. "As my DCI said, this is really not looking good for you. The body parts of three murdered men were found in your house. You haven't given any explanation as to how they got there, so you can imagine why we can only assume you killed those men. This is a triple murder you're looking at. You'll probably go to prison for at least thirty years."

"More like fifty," Chalmers corrected him. "So you'll maybe be out when you're eighty. If you live that long. What were those body parts doing in your house?"

"No comment."

"Tell us about the photograph," Yang Chu decided to steer the interview in another direction. "The one with you and Hal in Tibet. It's an amazing photograph with the monastery lit up by the sun. When was that taken?"

Penelope Slyper raised her head and stared at him. Her eyes were puffy and bloodshot and the piercings appeared to be threatening to pop out.

"Miss Slyper," Yang Chu urged. "When was that photo taken."

She exhaled a huge sigh. "I have no idea."

"You must remember roughly when you were in Tibet."

"I've never been to Tibet," she informed him. "The furthest I've been away from York is Greece. I've never been to Tibet."

"How do you explain the photo?"

"I'm not in the photograph," she said. "It's not me in that photo, it's Heidi."

CHAPTER FORTY EIGHT

Smith finished his third beer. His phoned was beeping on the table to tell him he'd received another message. He looked at the screen to see if it was a reply from Whitton but it was from Yang Chu again. He put the phone down and went upstairs to have a shower. He made the water as hot as he could bear and stood under the scolding jets until he couldn't take any more. When he got out and looked at himself in the mirror his whole face was red. He splashed some cold water on his face and dried himself. He dressed and went back downstairs. He took another beer outside to the back garden. Theakston and Fred were nowhere to be seen – they were clearly still busy digesting all the food Smith had given them.

His next-door-neighbour had gone. Smith sighed – he would quite like to talk to him again. He could hear the sound of his phone ringing inside the house.

"Leave me alone," Smith looked up at the sky. "Why can't everybody just leave me alone?"

He lit a cigarette and took a sip of beer. Then his thoughts turned to what they'd found inside Penelope Slyper's sideboard. The rotting hands, the bulging eyeballs and what had to be the preserved penis of Peter Ashe's were not something you found every day, but Smith felt oddly detached from the whole thing. He smiled inwardly when he thought about Grant Webber's reaction when he opened up the black jar. He wished he could have been there when Webber discovered what the jar contained.

Smith could hear that the snoring competition was over as soon as he went back inside the house. He was glad - he'd never heard snoring so loud. Both dogs ambled into the kitchen and Theakston nudged the door to indicate he wanted to go outside. Smith let them both out and closed the door behind them. He went back into the living room and turned on the television. The early edition of the news was about to begin.

* * *

"Interview with Penelope Slyper resumed, 17:10," Chalmers said. "Miss Slyper, let's see if we can get to the bottom of this shall we? We know the body parts found inside your house belong to the three men who were murdered this week. The penis in the jar belonged to your brother-in-law for goodness' sake. What I want to know is how did they get there?"

"No comment."

Penelope Slyper was starting to give Chalmers a headache.

"*No comment* isn't a reply that is going to do you any favours," he said. "*No comment* is two words that are going to ensure you spend the rest of your life behind bars. Why were these body parts inside your house?"

"No comment."

"Penelope," Yang Chu said. "The man in the photograph, this Hal bloke, do you know him?"

"Not very well."

"Does he live here in York?"

Chalmers frowned at him. Yang Chu nodded to indicate this line of questioning was going somewhere.

"Penelope?" Yang Chu urged.

"He's just moved here," she said.

"And you don't know him very well but Heidi does? Is that right?"

"They met while she was travelling – they lost touch for a while but then he must have contacted her again. She worships him for some reason."

"What do you mean she worships him?"

"He thinks he's some kind of Guru. You know the type – preaching about this and that. Some people fall for that kind of thing."

"And Heidi fell for it?" Yang Chu said. "Is that what you're saying?"

"I tried to stop her. I tried to tell her to keep away from him, but he had her under some kind of spell. I tried to stop her."

She started to cry again. Yang Chu waited for her to finish.

Chalmers looked like he was about to say something, but Yang Chu gave him a subtle shake of the head. They were making headway and the DCI's gruff approach wasn't what they needed right now.

"Penelope," Yang Chu said. "What did you try to stop?"

"When I heard about Peter, I knew it was Hal. And I knew Heidi was involved."

"You knew what?" Yang Chu wanted something less vague for the record.

"I knew Hal had killed Peter. And I knew Heidi had a hand in it."

"Do you know how they did it?"

"Not at first. Heidi didn't say. But after the third one I made her tell me. She didn't want to go back to the house where... You know, where she found Peter, and I said she could stay with me but only if she told me everything."

"What did she tell you?" Yang Chu knew they were getting somewhere.

"Heidi told me that Hal had had some kind of revelation. Some divine inspiration from a higher place is the way he described it. He thought there were demons everywhere. In everyone and he believed his purpose here on earth was to eradicate these demons. His words. He believed that God wasn't what was needed. God was old hat. Heidi told me he asked her to bug the confessional so that he could hear the confessions and he would then give absolution correctly."

"By chopping off body parts?" Yang Chu said. "And then murdering them?"

"Heidi believed it. She believed Hal was doing the right thing and these men were being saved."

"Miss Slyper," Chalmers couldn't keep quiet any longer. "You knew about these killings and yet you kept quiet. You let them carry on."

"Heidi is my sister," Penelope said. "What could I do? I tried to stop her, but she wouldn't listen. She's my sister. What would you have done?"

Dragged her down to the nearest police station myself, Chalmers thought, although he'd never got on with his own sister.

"Do you know where Heidi is now?" Yang Chu asked.

"I haven't seen her since this morning," Penelope replied. "What's going to happen now?"

"We're going to find your sister," Chalmers said. "And we're going to find this Hal. Then we're going to arrest them and they're going to go to jail for a very long time. As for you, I'm still debating whether to have you up as an accessory to murder."

"I didn't kill anybody."

"No," Chalmers said. "But you knew about it and you did nothing about it."

"Heidi is my sister," Penelope said once more. "She's my sister."

"Did Heidi say anything about where she was going?" Yang Chu asked.

"She just said she had to go out. There was something she needed to do."

"And you don't know what that was?"

"Something Hal discovered at work. A sinner who needed their help. Someone with demons to take away."

"Interview with Penelope Slyper finished, 17:28," Chalmers said and turned off the machine.

"Do you think she was telling the truth?" Yang Chu asked Chalmers in the canteen.

Chalmers had arranged for every available police officer to join a wide scale search for Heidi Ashe and her sidekick, Harry.

"I think she was," the DCI replied. "Her sister and this Hal or Harry or whatever he likes to call himself have been in it together. It makes sense. Harry listens to the confessions, Heidi watches the church and follows the man who's confessed and then Harry carries out the murder. It's quite ingenious really."

"Do you think we'll find them?"

"Of course. They must know we're on to them by now and that means they'll panic. And when people panic they slip up. We'll have them by the end of the day, you mark my words. I just hope they're found before another body turns up. I didn't like what Penelope said about another sinner."

"She said it was something Hal discovered at work," Yang Chu said. "If Webber's Harry is our killer, what did he discover at work?"

"The police force is full of sinners," Chalmers joked.

"You don't think..."

"Think what?"

"What if this something he discovered at work has something to do with a police detective's indiscretion with one of his colleagues?"

He took out his phone and brought up Smith's number.

CHAPTER FORTY NINE

Smith's phone rang for the twentieth time and he gave up. He picked it up and was about to answer it when it went dead. The last caller was Yang Chu. Smith called him back.

"What the hell is going on?" he asked. "Why can't you just leave me alone?"

"Didn't you get my message?" Yang Chu said. "About it not being Penelope Slyper in that photo?"

"So what?" Smith said. "We found the body parts in her house. What's the problem?"

"Her sister put them there. Heidi and Harry Grimes were in it together. Penelope told us everything. Heidi bugged the church and Harry listened in. Heidi followed the victim, told Harry where they lived and he went in and killed them."

"I still don't know what you want me to do about it," Smith said. "Put the word out – organise a search. They'll be found. I've done my bit."

The doorbell rang and Smith frowned.

"What now?"

"Excuse me?" Yang Chu said.

"I have to go – there's someone at the door. I'll see you tomorrow."

"Don't answer the door," Yang Chu said but Smith had already ended the call.

Webber's technician was standing outside when Smith opened the door. Smith looked him up and down but the split second he took in doing so was a split second too long. He watched as whatever Harry was holding in his hand made contact with his arm. Then he felt a slight burning sensation in his upper arm. He tried to lash out but his arm was already numb. Harry pushed him inside. Smith's whole body now felt numb and his legs no longer seemed to work. He collapsed to the ground. He felt himself being dragged into the living room and pushed onto the sofa. He could hear the dogs barking outside in the back garden.

"It's time," Harry said and took something out from inside his coat. He unwrapped the Kila knife and placed it carefully on the coffee table. "It's exquisite isn't it?" Harry said.

Smith tried to say something but his whole face was numb.

"I bought a dozen from a monk in Tibet," Harry told him. "It was a hassle to get them here, but it was worth it. I thought a dozen would be enough, but it appears I misjudged mankind's capacity to sin."

"You're insane," Smith meant to say, but it came out like, *youth ithen.*

Harry picked up Smith's phone and used Smith's fingerprint to open it. He swiped a few times and took out his own phone. He tapped away and shortly afterwards Smith's phone beeped to indicate he'd received a message.

"I'll let you read yours." Harry opened the messages. "Your absolution." The phone beeped again. Harry held the screen in front of Smith's face. "Read."

Smith saw that the most recent message was from Whitton.

I need time. I need time to think. Don't contact me again. I'll contact you.

"Did you read it?"

Smith nodded.

"Good. The Kila will take your demons, but that's not enough. You have to give *me* something. I have to take something to keep me moving on. Something to show me I'm getting closer to my own enlightenment. Do you understand?"

Smith nodded again even though he had no idea what this maniac was talking about.

"You have sinned," Harry took a knife with a serrated blade from his coat pocket. "And now demons feed from you. The demons in your heart will soon be damned to an eternity inside the walls of the Kila. But there are demons the Kila cannot contain so I will take them for you."

Smith thought about Laura. He could smell her scent. He thought about Whitton.

I'll contact you.

It was something, at least.

Harry held the knife up and inspected the blade. The he started mumbling words that had no meaning. They sounded like no language Smith had ever heard before. The knife was against Smith's neck and Harry held it there. "The anesthetic will be starting to wear off by now," he said.

For a split second their eyes met and then Smith felt a burning sensation under his chin. Then it was as if someone had drawn a thick curtain and shut off all the light in the world.

CHAPTER FIFTY

When Yang Chu and Chalmers burst into Smith's living room, Harry Grimes was holding a knife against Smith's neck. Smith's eyes were closed and Chalmers feared they were already too late. Yang Chu grabbed Harry by the hair and yanked his head back. Harry lunged with the knife but Yang Chu dodged and landed a right hook just under his chin. Chalmers followed up with a left to the cheek. Harry was still on his feet and he hadn't released the knife. Chalmers spotted the Kila dagger on the coffee table and picked it up. Harry slashed the air with the knife and Yang Chu felt a sting on his face as the tip sliced into his cheek. Smith still hadn't moved.

Harry was still waving the knife about wildly and Chalmers and Yang Chu didn't dare come too close. Yang Chu dropped low and with one sweep he kicked Harry's legs from under him. Harry fell onto the sharp point of the Kila dagger Chalmers was holding. The long thin knife entered his chest and effortlessly pierced his heart. Harry took hold of the ornate handle and gasped at it. He took two or three painful breaths and stopped moving.

Smith opened his eyes. His neck was painful and he could feel blood trickling under his shirt down his chest.

"I told you not to answer the door," Yang Chu said. "When are you going to start listening?"

"Probably never," Smith said. "What happened to your face?"

"A mere flesh wound," Yang Chu said and smiled.

"Your neck is bleeding," Chalmers said. "I'd better call for an ambulance. They can have a look at Yang Chu's flesh wound too."

"What happened?" Smith asked him.

"Your friend there was about to kill you," Chalmers pointed to the lifeless form of Harry Grimes. "Looks like we got here just in time."

Smith tried to get to his feet but his legs were still numb.

"Stay there," Chalmers said. "I'll organise that ambulance."

"We got Heidi Ashe," Yang Chu told him. "They found her at home. She didn't even put up a fight."

"That's something at least."

Smith looked at Harry Grimes. "That is one fucked up individual. "He told me he was going to imprison my demons in that knife."

"He'd need more than one of those knives for all your demons."

"You'd better inform Webber you've killed his technician."

Yang Chu started to laugh. Smith and Chalmers both stared at him.

"Sorry," Yang Chu said. "I'm just thinking of the look on Webber's face earlier."

"What are you talking about?" Smith said.

"He opened the jar. Grant Webber has seen many things and I doubt there's much that can upset him, but his face when he looked in that jar and realised he was looking at Peter Ashe's shrivelled-up todger was priceless."

THE END

Printed in Great Britain
by Amazon